SILVER LADY

SILVER LADY

LINDA GEORGE

FIVE STAR

An imprint of Thomson Gale, a part of The Thomson Corporation

Detroit • New York • San Francisco • New Haven, Conn. • Waterville, Maine • London

Copyright © 2007 by Linda George.

Thomson Gale is part of The Thomson Corporation.

Thomson and Star Logo and Five Star are trademarks and Gale is a registered trademark used herein under license.

Set in 11 pt. Plantin.

LIBRARY OF CONGRESS CATALOGING-IN-PUBLICATION DATA

George, Linda.
   Silver lady / Linda George. — 1st ed.
    p. cm.
   ISBN-13: 978-1-59414-613-8 (alk. paper)
   ISBN-10: 1-59414-613-6 (alk. paper)
   1. Colorado—Fiction. I. Title.
PS3557.E489S55 2007
813'.54—dc22   2007017294

First Edition. First Printing: October 2007.

Published in 2007 in conjunction with Tekno Books.

Printed in the United States of America on permanent paper
10 9 8 7 6 5 4 3 2 1

SILVER LADY

CHAPTER ONE

Wyoming, 1882

She stared down the barrel of a Colt .45.

"Don't move." The voice behind the gun was deep, gravelly, and dead serious.

On her knees, where she'd fallen into a clump of stickery brush, Kate Mathison closed her eyes and prayed the only prayer she knew. She screamed when the bullet whizzed past her left ear, leaving a trail of heat and powder on her cheek, then collapsed into the dust.

"It's all right, ma'am. The rattler's dead . . . afraid your husband is, too. I'm real sorry, ma'am."

Her husband? What was he talking about? The rattlesnake had spooked their horses . . . she fell . . . Ben! Kate struggled to her feet and stumbled over to where her brother lay face down on the rocky ground. Her sobs were bitter, angry, desperate.

"Ben, you can't be dead, you just can't—"

"His neck—"

"You shot him, didn't you? You killed my brother!"

"Your brother?" His forehead creased, then eased a mite. "Ma'am, I crested that hill and saw your brother lying on the ground and you beside him. When I saw that snake—but then you raised up and the snake coiled again. I think your brother broke his neck when he fell."

Kate bit her bottom lip and tried not to cry. The grief boiling inside her would have to wait. Right now, she had to think about staying alive and getting to Silverton.

She'd accused this man unfairly—after he'd saved her life. She'd have to apologize . . . when she could speak without sobbing.

The stranger's eyes were mere slits against the afternoon sun. "You can look for yourself, ma'am. I fired one shot. Your brother's body has no bullet in it. Just that mark on his left arm."

Kate looked at the wound, puckering red, darkening from the venom. The snake had left its ugly mark on Ben after he fell. No amount of crying or accusing would change it.

"Sorry." Kate straightened her sunbonnet, then wiped her eyes and face on the hem of her skirt. "I guess I—" She tried to stand, but her knees wouldn't take the weight. Slumping back, she sat for another minute, hoping her head would clear.

He offered his hand. She took it and allowed him to help her to her feet. His eyes were as blue as the Wyoming sky above them. His hair, coarse and straight, fell across his forehead from under a dusty slouch hat, reminding her of ripening wheat. The concern in his eyes was entirely new to Kate. No one but Ben had ever been genuinely concerned about her before.

She thanked him again and straightened her skirt. He tipped his canteen onto a bandanna to dampen it, then handed it to her. She wiped her face, grateful for the coolness. Her throat tightened when he pulled a blanket from his pack and spread it gently over Ben's body.

"I'd better see if I can round up your horses, ma'am, before they wander off too far. Will you be all right here until I get back?"

"Of course I'll be all right. I've been taking care of myself all my life." She winced, hearing the tone of her voice. She'd snapped at a man who'd been nothing but kind to her. He had nothing to do with the ornery no-good sidewinders in the saloon in Sutterfield who'd treated her like dirt under their boots. This man—had he told her his name?—had been nicer to her than any man she'd ever met, other than Ben.

"I'm sorry. I didn't mean to snap. I appreciate all you've done."

He stepped into his saddle and headed toward the next rise.

Kate turned and stared at the shrouded body. Weeping for Ben—and for herself—she gave in to the scenes darting through her mind. Ben riding a horse for the first time. Ben carrying water, tumbling down the hill when the buckets began to slosh. Ben telling her when he was only a child that he'd never marry as long as she was a maiden lady, that he'd stay with her as long as she lived, even if she never had the mind to take a husband at all.

But Ben had taken a wife, a lovely young girl with laughing eyes and ebony hair. He'd been happier than ever in his life. Then he lost her, three weeks ago, in childbirth. Lost the baby, too. The funeral had to have been the saddest Sutterfield had ever seen, even for the respectable citizens of the community.

Sweet Ben. Gone to be with his wife and child. And, for the first time in her life, Kate Mathison was utterly alone in the world, stranded in the middle of Wyoming with a stranger who'd just saved her life. Fearful she might die from the pain raging inside her, she wept and wept, unable to fight the hopelessness squeezing the breath from her.

After a while, he came back with her horses and tied them to a branch. They lowered their heads to crop skimpy grass around their hooves. He pulled a short-handled shovel from his saddlebags and started digging Ben's grave.

She watched in silence, the tears gone for now, cried away along with any hope for a decent life she might have had before that snake crossed their paths.

The stranger laid Ben's body in the grave, still covered with the rough blanket. He stared at her for a minute. "Want to say a few words over the body?"

She shook her head, unable to speak.

He took off his hat and swatted it against his leg a couple of times, producing a cloud of dust, then cleared his throat.

"Lord, this is Ben. He died too soon. Take care of him, Lord. And take care of his sister. Amen."

Kate nodded, grateful to him for saying what she could not.

He filled the grave, then piled rocks on top. At the head, he made a taller pile for a headstone. Ben's hat lay on the ground near where he'd fallen. Kate fetched it, brushed some of the dust from the crown, then hung it on top of the pile.

They stood in silence for a moment. Wiping her forehead with one sleeve, Kate sat down in the meager shade of a clump of the wiry bushes dotting the dry landscape. Knee-high grass, usually abundant in Wyoming, was scarce here. Lack of rain had stunted its growth, the same as around Sutterfield.

The stranger sat down beside her, keeping a discreet distance. "I'm afraid the saddlebags came untied. I couldn't find them. Where were you headed?"

She hesitated, afraid to tell him the truth. "New Mexico."

"That's a long way from here."

"We got a wire from my pa. He asked us to come. We haven't seen him in a long time." She didn't tell him anything about the silver mine or the claim jumpers. All that silver seemed worthless now, compared to Ben's life.

The stranger shook his head and closed his eyes. "That's real poor luck, ma'am. Real poor." He swiped his sleeve across his eyes, pushed his hat back on his head, and gave her a sad smile.

Kate brushed her hair back from her face. "You haven't told me your name."

"Drew Kingman."

"That short for Andrew?"

"Yep. Pleased to make your acquaintance."

"Same here. I'm Kate Mathison." She held out a grimy hand. He touched her fingertips lightly in response.

How silly. Formal introductions, sitting under a scratchy bush in the middle of Wyoming next to a fresh grave. Kate's throat closed again. She fought the tears unsuccessfully.

Drew hesitated, then reached for her shoulder and pulled her against him. Damn, but she was a handsome woman. Piles of blond hair, blowing every which way in the dry autumn wind, dusky blue eyes, and skin like August peaches, blushed by too much sun, yet obviously pale beneath. Damn, but he wished he could've gotten here a few minutes sooner.

Her stomach rumbled.

Drew loosened his hold on her reluctantly. She smiled shyly, wiping her eyes with the hem of her skirt. The gesture left streaks of mud on her blistered cheeks.

Without thinking, Drew swiped at the mud with his thumbs, stopping only when he realized her cheeks were getting redder by the minute. "Dirt. On your face. Gone now." He coughed nervously, then headed for his horse and the saddlebags. He pulled out a bundle, unwrapped it, then handed her a piece of beef. Not jerky, exactly, but still dry and tough. "I'm sorry I don't have something more tasty. It'll fill an empty belly, though."

"Thank you kindly." She accepted the piece and bit off a small corner, appreciating the pungent flavor of the roasted beef. Kate could hardly remember a day of her life when he hadn't been hungry.

Everything she owned had been in the lost saddlebags—her other dress, what little food they had left, and her only quilt. She'd made it herself, from a bundle of rags left in a trash heap behind the millinery shop in Sutterfield where she'd worked these past five years. At least she still had the wire from Pa in her pocket. She'd never get there in time now. Those jumpers would take everything. They might even kill Pa before she had a chance to see what he looked like. Last time she saw him, she'd been five years old. Memories from that long ago weren't worth much.

She took the opportunity to study Drew Kingman more closely. Older than she, but not more than five years. Fairly decent looking by any woman's standards. He didn't have the stink of a buffalo hunter. His pants and Texas-style spurs might make him a drover.

The breeze on her face felt good, drying sweat, carrying away some of the shock and pain. She wanted to feel numb. Drew reached for his canteen, wiped the rim clean with his bandanna, then handed it to her.

"Thanks." She drank her fill of the water, surprisingly cool and sweet, then handed the canteen back to him.

Drew took a long pull, screwed the cap back on, then hung it over his saddle horn. "Laramie's just south of here. I'm heading that way if you'd like to ride along. I won't leave you alone out here."

"Thank you kindly. I'm not keen on the idea of being alone just yet."

She stood by Ben's grave for a long moment, then stepped into her saddle, groaning at new soreness in her bruised muscles. "Good-bye, Ben," she whispered, then turned the big roan and nudged him with her heels.

Drew waited patiently on his palomino, leading Ben's bay. She kicked her horse harder and caught up, riding astride instead of sidesaddle. The fact impressed him. Once, when nobody was looking, he'd twisted his knee around the saddle horn, to see if that was a comfortable way to ride. The stupid stunt had almost crippled him. He managed to get his legs straightened out just before he would've been caught. There was no way he'd ever insist a woman ride sidesaddle, no matter what was said about the ones who did.

"Ready?" He felt as solemn as she looked, having to leave her brother behind.

"I'm ready, Mr. Kingman."

He had to give her credit for strength and perseverance. She'd cried a well full of tears, but he couldn't fault her for that. Pulling herself together demonstrated courage he'd never seen in women. He'd have to tell her, in the morning before he left for Denver, how much he admired her spirit.

He selected an easy pace. Kate lagged a bit behind, trying to sort all the feelings darting through her brain like bees in a honeysuckle vine. Nothing made any sense now. She finally gave up trying to sort things out and let her mind go blank. The only thing she knew for sure was how lucky she'd been that Drew Kingman had come along when he did. Otherwise, she might have been killed by the rattler, and they would've lain there until someone found them. Life, even one as miserable as hers had been at times, was precious. Ben's son never had the chance to know that. Someday, if Kate had a child, she'd make sure it was loved and nurtured, respected and treated fairly. Her child would have everything she'd grown up without.

She pulled her secondhand blue serge traveling dress closer together in the front over the white muslin waist. The wind had become decidedly cooler with the lowering of the sun. The horse's plodding lulled her into a restless half-sleep, while the sun sank in the sky, shadows stretching into the evening to come.

They rode into town at dusk. Kate roused from restless dozing and looked around. Not much here. In fact, this town appeared smaller than Sutterfield. The setting sun blazed red-orange, splashing brilliant colors over wispy clouds hovering slightly above the horizon. The drab clapboard buildings, darkened by gathering night shadows, gave Kate a chill. Too much like Sutterfield.

Drew stopped about halfway down the street in front of a tall building and waited for her to catch up. Kate didn't have money for room and board. What little money they'd brought with them had disappeared with the saddlebags.

"I'll pay for your room, Miss Mathison, if you'll allow me to do it. With losing your brother and all, and your saddlebags—"

"I appreciate the offer, Mr. Kingman, but I would never think of burdening you further." Her head swam with dizziness. She clutched the saddle horn, hoping she could get down from the horse without falling.

"It's no burden, ma'am. I'd be proud to do it in memory of your brother."

He'd given her an easy way to accept. "Put that way, I don't see how I could refuse." Her legs had stiffened. Drew reached to help her down. His hands on her waist lingered a brief moment when he set her on the ground. Then she realized he doubted she could stand on her own.

He kept one hand on her elbow, to steady her up the porch steps. The stiffness hadn't settled only into her legs. Her back screamed, her shoulders protested every move.

Drew held the rough wooden door open for her, waiting patiently as she went inside. She didn't have the energy to survey the front rooms. Random thoughts swirled through her mind. A hot bath in a real bathtub. Extra charge. No money for bed or board. No money for anything. A bed. Heavenly. Her mind screamed for sleep.

Drew went to the front desk and signed the register with a goose quill pen, hoping Kate wouldn't fall during the brief time he'd let go of her arm. He saw her start to sag and eased one arm around her, pulling her close to him while he wrote her name beneath his.

"Thank you kindly," she mumbled, slumping against him, apparently half asleep.

"Upstairs, first and second doors," the hotel keeper told them. "I'm Joe. You need anything, holler."

Drew tried to rouse Kate enough to walk up the stairs. She was out on her feet. He scooped her into his arms and headed up the stairs. Her head lolled back over his arm, her mouth sagged open, and a low snore erupted from her throat. Shifting her toward him, her cheek finally nestled into his shoulder, closing her mouth. Joe clumped up the stairs behind them.

When they got to the first door, Joe pushed ahead to open it. Drew told him to pull the covers down, then laid her on the big feather bed as gently as he could manage. He unlaced her shoes and tugged them off her feet, then tucked her legs under the quilt, covering her only halfway since it was still warm in the room. He didn't want her to get too hot. When he opened the window a couple of inches, it sagged back to its rut in the frame.

"Is there a prop for this window?"

"On the floor."

Drew chose the shorter of the chunks of wood lying beneath the window and propped it open. A cool breeze freshened the room enough to satisfy him.

She was wearing too many clothes, but he wasn't about to undress her. "You have a wife, Joe?"

"Yep."

"Would you ask her to come up here and take off most of Miss Mathison's clothes, so she'll sleep better?" He pulled a dollar from his pocket and handed it to him.

"I'll tell her." He pocketed the money.

Kate's eyes fluttered open. "I want you . . . to know . . . how much . . . I appre . . . appre . . .". Her lashes fluttered down, mouth open, and her soft snoring resumed.

Drew made a wry face at Joe. "Hard day. We buried her

brother just north of here. She's plumb tuckered." He reached to nudge Kate's chin upward, but it sagged immediately. He gave up and followed Joe to the door.

"I'll get Meg." Joe tromped down the stairs.

Glancing at Kate lying there on the bed, Drew couldn't help smiling. He felt as sorry for her as any woman he'd ever known. But she had something . . . different. Something other women didn't have. Guts.

CHAPTER TWO

When Kate next opened her eyes, she had no idea where she was or how she'd gotten there. A slight woman with kind eyes sat beside the bed, bathing her face and arms with a wet cloth. Wrinkles in her ruddy face turned to laugh lines when she smiled.

"Just take it easy," the woman said in a calm, soothing voice. "You've run yourself to exhaustion, you have. I wanted to get you cleaned up a bit."

"Who are you?" Kate's tongue felt dry and twice its normal size.

"Meg McGruder. My husband and I own this hotel." Meg helped Kate lean forward enough to sip some fragrant tea, then eased her back onto the pillow. "It's called the Prancing Horse. Do you remember getting here last night?"

"Last night?"

"You passed out cold at the front desk. Mr. Kingman carried you up here and put you in bed, dirt and all. He couldn't stand the thought of your sleeping in all those clothes, and asked me to help you out of them. I don't think you knew what was going on, though. Mumbled a little, but nothing I could make out."

Now that she thought about it, Kate realized she had on only her long skirt chemise and red flannel winter drawers. She didn't remember being undressed at all. "What time is it?"

"Nigh on three o'clock. But don't you worry none. That nice Mr. Kingman has paid your room and board for a whole week.

When you're up to it, I'll heat some water so you can have a bath. He said you've come a long way. Didn't say where from, though." She glanced down. "I'm real sorry to hear about your brother, God rest his soul."

Ben. Memories came rushing back, heavy and painful. Tears spilled from her eyes. "I'm sorry," she sobbed. "I should do my crying when I'm alone."

"Nonsense. You need to let it out, child. It ain't good to keep all that grieving inside. Let it all come out, so it won't poison your soul." She took the basin of water and closed the door gently on her way out.

Kate squeezed her eyes shut, crying for Ben, and for the predicament she'd gotten herself into. Her tears soaked into the pillow as thoughts of her mother mingled with those of Ben.

She'd loved rocking in Ma's favorite chair, listening to her tell stories or sing little songs before bedtime every night. Happy times. When Ma died in the fire that took their house and the barn, leaving them orphaned and homeless, a huge empty place had opened up in Kate that remained to this day. Even Ben couldn't fill it. If that old lantern hadn't fallen from the table, catching the rag run on fire—But wishing things could've been different changed nothing. Through the years, she'd thought about it thousands of times, trying to figure out a way she could've kept the lantern from falling. But every time she'd come to the same conclusion. No one could've predicted what happened, or prevented the fire. An accident, pure and simple. An accident that changed their lives forever.

She turned her thoughts to her current situation. Meg said Drew Kingman had paid a week's room and board. He had to be the kindest man she'd ever known. And a fine gentleman. The type of man Kate could never hope to—

A timid knock at the door produced the man she vaguely remembered from the front desk last night.

"Meg says you can come downstairs to eat, or she'll brang you a bowl. Which is it?"

Kate thought about her dress and how it must look after days on horseback, falling into the dirt, then more riding.

"I'd love to come downstairs, but I don't have any clothes to wear."

"Oh." He backed out and closed the door.

About five minutes later, Kate heard the sound of footsteps on the stairs. A light knock, then Meg came in. "I'm sorry. I plumb forgot. I've washed your dress. It's hanging out back to dry. If you'd like, you can wear one of my eldest daughter's dresses till yours dries. There are three in the wardrobe. Take your pick."

"Thank you. Is this her room?"

"It was. She died two years ago, God rest her soul."

"I'm terribly sorry. Are you sure you want me to wear one of her dresses?"

Meg smiled, her eyes bright with tears. "You remind me a little of her. I'd appreciate seeing her dresses put to some use again."

"Thank you. I'll take care of them, I promise."

"Need some help?"

"I don't know. Let me try." Sitting on the side of the bed produced some groans from the effort, followed by a minute or so of sitting still to allow her head to clear. When she tried to stand, she felt weak, but managed to leave the bed and walk without wobbling too much. Meg kept one hand protectively on Kate's arm for balance.

"You'll feel better once you've eaten some stew and corn-bread."

"It seems like ages since I last ate." Her stomach rumbled at the thought of hot food.

"Let's get you dressed, then, and downstairs."

Three dresses hung on nails inside the massive wardrobe. A blue calico caught her eye. She pulled it out, shook it hard a couple of times, then tried it on, with Meg's help. It proved a bit tight, but wouldn't have been with her corset.

"I ought to be wearing my corset, but the tortuous thing was too uncomfortable to wear while riding."

"Don't worry a bit. I gave up wearing those things years ago. They pinch."

Once Kate got to Silverton, she'd buy a new one, with lace, ruffles, and embroidery at the bodice. If she didn't get back to wearing one soon, her waist would swell until she couldn't be comfortable being seen in public.

"Do you have a hairbrush, Meg?"

Meg handed her one from the chiffonnier. Kate tried to pull it through her tangled hair, but couldn't. Her scalp felt gritty with dirt. A glance at her pillow showed a dirty spot where she'd lain. Embarrassment warmed her cheeks. In the mirror, her hair was the same color as the scrawny tabby cat that hung around the saloon in Sutterfield.

Tears threatened again, but for a different reason this time. She couldn't be seen like this in a nice hotel.

"What is it, child?"

"My hair. It's too dirty to be seen by respectable folk. And the rest of me is dirty, too. I've even soiled the sheets and pillowslip. I'm so ashamed."

Meg gave her an assuring smile. "Don't you fret, now. I'll heat some water. You stay right here in your room. I'll get Joe to bring the washtub and you can have a bath before you come downstairs."

Kate dabbed at her nose and eyes with a soiled handkerchief from her bodice. "I hate being such a bother."

"It's no bother! You just rest and I'll get that water on to heat. And remember, child, being dirty isn't a sin. Not caring is the sin. It won't be long, I promise."

Kate's stomach grumbled again.

"I'll send up a bowl of stew with the tub."

She hugged Kate briefly and left, her dainty feet pattering down the stairs.

Joe brought the stew first, then the tub. Kate sat on the edge of the bed, dipping hot cornbread into the thick broth, savoring every delectable bite.

A few minutes later, Joe knocked again, with one bucket of hot water and one of cold. "Meg's heating more. Soap's on the sideboard."

"I can't thank you enough, Mr. McGruder."

"Joe. You're welcome." He left without another word.

Kate poured the hot and cold water together into the tub, found the soap, scented with lavender, and scrubbed her hair first, then the rest of her. Before long the water was dingy. More knocking. Meg this time. "Here's more hot water. Want me to bring it in?"

"Yes, please! But give me a minute. I'm not decent." She grabbed her chemise and held it in front of her to maintain some modesty.

Meg peeked in, then opened the door wider for the water. "Joe's downstairs. It's just me." She came in with the first bucket, then went back for the second. "Pour the dirty water out that window and use this to finish up."

Kate was embarrassed for Meg to see how dirty she'd been. She peered outside to make sure no one was beneath the window, then dumped the water.

Meg sat primly on the edge of the bed. "I had no idea your hair was that light. Looks real purty."

"Thank you." Still clutching the chemise, Kate didn't know what to do next.

Meg got up from the bed. "When you're dressed, come on

downstairs. There's plenty of stew and cornbread left if you're still hungry."

"It was so delicious, I practically ate the bowl, too. I'll be down before too long, I promise."

"Take your time." Before closing the door, she looked back. "Mr. Kingman asked after you a while ago. He'll be around later to say good-bye."

The thought of seeing Drew again excited her in an unusual way. She'd never looked forward to seeing any man, other than Ben. But he was coming to say good-bye. Why should that make her feel empty again?

More dirty skin needed scrubbing. Best get to it.

When she'd finished her bath and dumped the rest of the water out the window, she tried the brush again. Her throat tightened with sudden memories of Ben. He'd always told her, after she'd had a bath and washed her hair, that she looked "plumb nice." She pushed the memories down, into the deepest part of herself—that big empty space—knowing it would take a long time before she could think of Ben with anything but pain and sadness. At least he was with his wife and child. That thought made her smile.

Dressed in the blue calico dress, she stepped into the hallway at half past five, feeling more presentable than she had in weeks. Meg met her at the kitchen door.

"Lawsy, child, you're prettier than a newborn calf. Ain't she, Joe?"

Joe looked up from a newspaper, stared at Kate through wire rim spectacles, and said, "Yep." He immediately went back to his paper.

"Have you lived here a long time, Mr. McGruder?"

"Joe. Yep."

"Have you always had the hotel?"

"Yep."

So much for polite conversation. "The stew was delicious, Meg. You're a good cook."

Obviously pleased, Meg wiped her floured hands on her apron. "Do you like to cook?"

"When I have the chance. I love being in the kitchen." Her favorite kitchen had been at home, with Ma bustling about, frying pancakes and bacon for breakfast, just as she'd been doing when the fire broke out. She'd swung the milk pail up onto the table and hit the lantern. It crashed to the floor, spilling kerosene everywhere, catching the rug on fire. Ma pushed Kate out the front door, then went to find Ben. But he was out back in the barn, tending a new foal. Ma kept looking until it was too late to escape. Ben managed to get a few of the animals out of the barn before it caught . . .

"Thinking about your brother?"

Kate snapped out of her thoughts and gasped at the grief flooding through her. "Yes. I miss him terribly."

"I know just how you feel. There are times when I expect my daughter to come through that front door. 'Course, she never does." Meg stared at nothing for a moment. "I 'spect Mr. Kingman anytime. You can wait in the parlor, if you want." She went back to the kitchen.

To the right of the front door was a long room. A long dining table took up the near end of the room, with two divans at the far end by the fireplace, for conversation after meals, she assumed. A kerosene lamp sat next to a faded picture of George and Martha Washington in a little easel on a table with clawed feet. Kate glanced at every item in the room, giving herself something to do while she waited for Drew Kingman. What had he called this town?

"Joe?"

He looked up.

"What town is this?"

"Laramie, Wyoming." Back to the paper.

So, she was still in Wyoming. How long would it take to get to Silverton from here? She and Ben had covered about thirty-five miles a day on fairly flat ground. She knew practically nothing about the terrain in Colorado, except that's where the Rocky Mountains were. Did they cover the whole state, she wondered? Exactly where in Colorado was Silverton? Winter was several months away, but the mountains might be covered in snow in summer, as well as winter.

The front door opened and closed. Drew Kingman went to the front desk, then, after a gesture from Joe, came into the parlor. She swallowed hard. He'd had a bath, too, and a shave. His clothes were anything but worn and dirty, as she vaguely remembered them from the day before.

He pulled a new black slouch hat from his head. His wheat-colored hair had been sheared and slicked down with tonic, just enough to make it stay in place. Parted just left of center, it lay in waves on either side. Kate reminded herself to breathe. Drew Kingman wasn't just pleasant to look at. In that get-up, with his face washed and clean-shaven, he was downright handsome.

"Miss Mathison. You're looking rested. Are you feeling better today?"

"I am, for a fact."

Drew twirled his hat in his hands. "Have you had supper yet?" He shined the toe of one freshly oiled boot on the back of his nankeen trousers, then looked to see if the oil had left a spot.

"I had some stew, but that was some time ago."

"I'd be pleased to take you to supper, ma'am." He shined the other boot, then straightened his brown sack coat and vest over the yellowish-brown trousers.

Kate felt a lump form in her throat. Such courtesy and respect. "I'd be pleased to have supper with you, Mr. Kingman." She smiled and wondered what she should do next. She remembered something Ma used to say, about feeling as nervous as a long-tailed cat in a room full of rocking chairs.

"Do you have a wrap? The place I have in mind is down the street a piece, and the wind tends to get a bit nippy after sundown."

"No, I'm afraid I don't."

Meg appeared at the door. "A wrap? There's a shawl upstairs. Joe'll get it for you. My, but don't you both look spiffy. Ain't he a sight, Kate?"

Kate blushed, but nodded. "You look very nice, Mr. Kingman." And he did. He really did.

"Uh . . . if we can get that wrap, we'll be going, Mrs. McGruder." Drew gave his hat another twirl.

"Joe! The blue one with the medallions! You two just wait right here." She turned toward the desk. "Joe!" He laid his paper on the desk and headed upstairs.

Kate had no idea what to do with herself while they waited, so she smiled at Drew, straightened her skirts, pulled at her sleeves, then studied the picture of George and Martha Washington until Joe reappeared with a crocheted shawl.

Kate swung it around her shoulders and crossed the ends in the front.

"Purty. You two have a nice evening, now, ya hear?"

"Thank you, Meg." Kate gave her a shy smile.

Drew held the door for Kate to go first. That odd sensation tingled through her again. *A lady.* He was treating her like a lady. If he had any idea of her upbringing, he'd no doubt treat her quite differently. She had no intention of telling him.

CHAPTER THREE

"It's this way." Drew walked between her and the dusty main street. "They serve supper until eight each evening."

"Do you live here in Laramie, Mr. Kingman?" She felt she should try to make pleasant conversation, the way she'd heard fine ladies do in Sutterfield, when they came to buy hats at the millinery where she'd worked. Everything she knew about being proper came from Eliza Branchfield's customers.

"No, ma'am. I'm staying at the Prancing Horse, same as you."

Should she remember that? She didn't.

A rider clopped down the street next to the wooden plank walkway. Drew moved closer to shield her from dust kicked up by the horse's hooves, but it swirled around them anyway.

Kate cleared her throat. He turned toward her and grinned. How very blue his eyes were. Her eyes were blue, too, but a completely different shade. Ben had always called hers smoky blue, like the sky after an afternoon thunderstorm. Drew Kingman's eyes were the azure of a cloudless summer day. She realized she was staring. A lady would never be caught staring. She pretended to be interested in something across the street.

Drew wanted to laugh out loud. The prim and proper Miss Mathison wanted him to think she was a lady, through and through. He wished she'd give it up and just be herself. Because the real Kate Mathison, the one behind all the prim and proper manners, was the woman he'd asked to supper. He hoped to coax her out from behind those manners and find out more about where she'd come from and the real reason she was going to see her father. He'd seen in her eyes she wasn't telling him everything about this little journey when she'd mentioned New Mexico.

They reached the café. Drew held the door for her again. Kate sighed with pleasure. This drover, if that's what he was, hadn't always been on a horse. His manners were refined and polished, as though he were used to escorting respectable ladies to fine restaurants. This restaurant couldn't exactly be called fine. At least she didn't think so, judging from the descriptions she'd heard of places in San Francisco and Denver. Still, it was a far sight better than the eating places in Sutterfield. Here, there were tablecloths and napkins. Fine enough for Kate.

Drew led the way to a table near the front windows, pulled out a high-back cane-bottom chair for her, adjusted the chair as she sat, then sat opposite. His paper collar, sitting atop his ruffled linen shirt, appeared a bit tight, judging from the way he kept inserting his finger to loosen it from time to time.

Kate thought about suggesting he undo the top button, but he'd also have to undo his black silk cravat, tucked neatly under the edges of the collar, and that might set the collar crooked. Not proper at all.

If Ben could only see her now, sitting with a real gentleman, about to have supper with him, worrying over what was proper and what wasn't. How her life had changed. She studied her escort carefully while he listened to the cook recite the menu. It didn't take long, since they had only three choices—beef, chicken, and pork.

Drew's hair waved over his forehead now, having relaxed somewhat, but it was still slicked back on the sides above full sideburns. Kate wondered if his hair felt as coarse as it appeared, or if the comb marks left there by the tonic just made it seem that way. His hair might be as soft as hers was tonight.

She twirled one blond curl falling over her shoulders. How long had it been since her hair had been this soft and sweet-smelling? The color was genuine again, too. Ben had called it summer sunshine.

Drew ordered a large beefsteak. Kate nodded, and he made it two. Cooking smells coming from the kitchen made her stomach fuss. She sipped water from a jelly jar glass and glanced around uncomfortably. Drew broke the awkward silence with a question.

"Where, exactly, are you from?"

"A small Montana town called Sutterfield. I was born there."

He nodded, but didn't ask more. Not ready yet to reveal the truth about her upbringing, she felt she could still practice conversing without revealing anything embarrassing.

"My father left us when I was five. My mother died in a fire, a year later. Ben and I—" She couldn't give away too much. "We lived with relatives until we received the wire saying Pa was alive. He actually wants to see us again." She'd better stop before she got confused and said something she'd rather keep to herself. She sipped water from the glass.

"How long since he left home?"

"Almost twenty years." Oh dear. Now he knew her age. She grabbed her water glass again and took several more sips. "Forgive me, Mr. Kingman. I don't mean to spoil the evening with idle chatter about myself and my family. Let's talk about you. Where are you from?"

"Texas."

She should've known. "Are you a cattleman?"

"From time to time." He didn't offer more, just smiled and drank about half of his water in two gulps.

The steaks arrived, so they took a break from conversation. Kate ate every bite of the meat in spite of its being quite tough in places. She also ate all of the boiled potatoes. After being half-empty most of her life, it felt wonderful to be completely full, twice in one day.

Drew watched her with interest and amusement. She'd put that steak away as though she had a hollow leg she had to fill. He wondered about the relatives she'd grown up with, and how well off they'd been. From the look of her, she'd never been the least bit rounded. Bones tended to jut from her, elbows and shoulders, with too little padding. Damn, but she'd cleaned up nice. He'd love to finger those curls falling around her face, shining like the sun. Damned fine woman, this Kate Mathison.

He swiped his lips with the napkin. "Most ladies pick around and leave their plates practically full, as though eating like a bird was something to be admired. I like to see a woman enjoy food right down to the last bite."

Kate felt a shudder of embarrassment, then dismissed it. Why shouldn't she eat if she were hungry? He'd never have to worry about her wasting good food for propriety's sake. Of course, she'd have to buy a larger corset in Silverton, but she could starve herself into a smaller size later. Much later.

"Thank you, Mr. Kingman. I enjoyed the beefsteak immensely. I agree, wasting food is a sin."

"Well, I didn't exactly say that, but I guess you're right." His smile spread slowly. He had perfectly white teeth with no gaps. A piece of steak dangled from between the front two.

Kate burst out laughing.

"Did I say something funny?"

"No. No. Not at all." She sipped more water, trying not to laugh.

He smiled again.

Trying to be discreet, she picked up her napkin and scrubbed at her front teeth a couple of times, then put the napkin back in her lap and smiled.

He laughed. After a quick scrub, he smiled again, wider than ever. "Better?"

"Perfect."

"You're a mighty handsome woman, Miss Mathison."

"Why, thank you, Mr. Kingman. You're mighty handsome yourself."

They laughed together. To Kate, it felt wonderful. Conversation wasn't the least bit difficult after that.

An hour later, back at the Prancing Horse, Kate didn't want Drew to leave, fearing, as Meg had suggested, he might be leaving for good. The thought of never seeing him again made her fidgety.

Drew asked if she'd like to sit in the parlor for a while.

"I'd like that very much." She tried, without success, to stifle a yawn. "I'm afraid I'm still tired from my fall, and all that's happened. Please excuse me."

"Of course. I shouldn't keep you, then."

He couldn't leave yet! She had to know him better! And she needed to practice being a lady with someone willing to endure her mistakes before she tried it on the general public.

She extended her hand as she'd seen the proper ladies of Sutterfield do so many times. "Thank you again for a most enjoyable evening and a fine meal. I truly hope we might do it again sometime."

Drew took her hand, wishing she'd drop the fancy lady talk and tell him what she thought, straight out. It would take time, though, and trust, neither of which he could afford to indulge at the moment. He had to leave for Denver first thing in the morning—the last thing he wanted to do right now—and get back to Texas as soon as he could. He had to explain to Jerome why his brother was dead—and why Drew had been forced to kill him.

"This evening has been my pleasure. And thanks again for alerting me to the steak between my teeth."

She burst out laughing. Good. That was more like the real Kate. It wouldn't take much to get her to drop those la-de-da ways and—He had to stop those thoughts. Such feelings were totally inappropriate, considering he'd never see this woman again after tomorrow. He offered his arm to escort her upstairs. She grinned at him all the way.

"Will I see you in the morning?"

Her smile, so wistful it tore at his heart, faded when he picked up her hand and squeezed her fingers gently. Did he detect a hint of pinkness in her cheeks?

"I'll come by before I leave town."

"You're leaving so soon?" Her smile wavered.

"I have business that can't wait."

"Of course. I've caused you enough delay already. Good night, Mr. Kingman, and thank you again for everything you've done for me. I'll be just fine. You needn't worry yourself about me in the least."

Such brave words, from a woman literally quaking in her shoes. Drew was tempted to hang around Laramie a few more days and see if he could get the real Kate Mathison to come out and stay. Tempting. Truly tempting.

Drew squeezed her fingers one last time, tipped his hat, and went next door to his own room.

Reluctantly, Kate went inside and closed the door, then pressed her ear to the wall, listening until she heard his door close. She flopped onto the soft feather bed and felt her muscles relax as they'd been begging to do for the past half hour.

Tomorrow she'd try to persuade him to stay in Laramie a little longer. But what legitimate reason did she have for wanting him to stay? She liked him. Really liked him. But she couldn't come straight out and say so, could she? Of course not. A lady would never be so bold.

She had to think about earning money to buy supplies for the rest of the trip. That meant getting a job. She could never cross the Rockies alone. A lady would never go anywhere alone, but Kate would go alone if it came to that. No way would she allow no-good, thieving claim jumpers to deprive her of the life she'd always dreamed of having. She'd still have it, if determination counted for anything. She just wouldn't have it as quickly as she'd hoped.

If only she had someone to go with her. Someone with manners and refinement. Someone with flashing white teeth with no gaps. Someone with eyes as blue as a clear Wyoming sky.

CHAPTER FOUR

Sunlight streamed through the crocheted lace curtains at daybreak the next morning and woke Kate. She stretched and found that some of the soreness had gone, but the stiffness had not. Her blue serge dress, washed and neatly pressed, hung on a nail on the back of the door.

Kate yawned sleepily, climbed down from the high four-poster bed, stepped onto the rag rug, then reached for the dress. The muslin waist hung there, too. The dress felt tight across the bosom, but it didn't squeeze her overly much. She'd been lucky to get a dress near the right size from the church ladies before leaving Sutterfield.

First things first this morning. Kate knew she had to convince Drew Kingman to take her to Silverton in exchange for nothing more than a promise that he'd be paid once they got there. At least she hoped he'd be paid. Surely, with her father's newly found wealth, he'd be willing to pay Drew for bringing his daughter all the way from Wyoming. But worrying about it now served no good purpose. She'd worry about it when the time came.

Kate left her room and went downstairs. She looked all around the parlor but Drew was nowhere to be seen. Kate peeked into the warm, fragrant kitchen. "Good morning."

Meg looked up from a dough board. A spot of flour decorated her nose. "Sleep well?"

"Like a rock."

"There's coffee if you want some."

"Thanks." Kate selected a cup from those sitting on the counter. Meg filled it to the brim. "Meg?"

"Yeah?"

"Have you seen Mr. Kingman this morning?"

"Checked out about half an hour ago."

A chill ran down Kate's back. "Checked out? He's leaving town, then?"

"Didn't say." Meg offered a bowl of brown sugar to Kate.

"I see." Kate spooned some sugar into her cup and stirred it, being careful not to slosh any on the floor.

"Didn't he mention anything to you last night about leaving?" Meg opened the oven door, used her skirt as a potholder, and took out a pan of biscuits. The tantalizing aroma filled the kitchen.

"No, he didn't say a word about it." Confound it! Now, she'd have no other choice but to find work and—

"Morning, everybody. Those biscuits sure do smell good, Mrs. McGruder." Kate recognized the voice before she ever turned around. Drew Kingman filled the doorway. He had on his traveling clothes.

"Mr. Kingman." Kate took a long, deep breath. So. She had a choice after all.

"I came to tell you good-bye, ma'am, and good luck. If there's anything else I can do for you before I leave—"

"As a matter of fact, there is," Kate said evenly. She took another sip of coffee.

"You two have a biscuit." Meg split two of the golden brown biscuits, slipped a chunk of butter inside each one, and handed them to Kate and Drew. Then she went about gathering up dirty dishes and dumped them into the washbasin.

"Thanks, Meg." Kate drizzled molasses onto the steaming biscuit, then ate it hungrily.

"Best I've tasted in a coon's age, Mrs. McGruder." Drew reached for the molasses and another biscuit. "Much obliged."

Meg grinned and attacked a greasy pan with gusto.

Drew finished the second biscuit, licked the molasses from his fingers, and wiped his hands on his jeans. Then he looked at Kate. "Shall we go into the parlor, Miss Mathison?"

Kate nodded and eased past him out of the kitchen. She could still smell his hair tonic, spicy and masculine. He must have gotten it at the barbershop yesterday. To Kate, it smelled even better than Meg's biscuits.

In the parlor, two gentlemen sat at the table at the far end, arguing about cattle prices. They didn't even look up when Kate and Drew came into the room.

Kate took a long, slow, deep breath and wondered again how she should phrase her question. Drew Kingman would have to be a fool to take her up on such a proposition, considering she hadn't even had the price of a meal or a room for the night, but she was determined to try, even if he laughed in her face.

They sat down at opposite ends of a gold brocade sofa that had been worn to threads on the arms and on the front edge. Kate straightened her dress over her knees and cleared her throat before beginning. When she looked up and saw Drew's eyes trained on her, she completely forgot what she had planned to say.

"You need something else, ma'am?" He kept looking away and back again, as though he were doing the asking instead of her. Or, maybe he was just interested in the price of cattle.

"I do, Mr. Kingman, and I believe you are the only person who might be able to help me with what I need."

"If I can, ma'am." He waited patiently, sat on the edge of the sofa, and twirled his new hat in his hands.

"As I told you, Mr. Kingman . . ." She couldn't keep on lying about her destination if she expected him to help her, but she didn't have to tell him about the silver mine. Not yet, anyway. "My father is desperately ill and my brother and I were going to see him one last time."

"Yes, ma'am, you told me." He quit looking away and just looked at her.

Kate glanced at her hands, twisting in her lap. "Well, I'm afraid I wasn't entirely honest about where my father is. You see, I didn't know you very well then and I was afraid—that is—I didn't know if I could trust you or not."

"I understand, ma'am. Where is your father?"

"In Colorado."

"Well, that'll make it a mite easier for you to get there before he dies. That is, if you start out now. If you don't, you won't make it through the Rockies before snow flies."

"I'm well aware of that fact, Mr. Kingman." Kate took another long, deep breath. "That is why I'm prepared to offer you a proposition."

"A proposition?" He dropped his hat on the crocheted runner on the table beside the sofa, then leaned toward her. "And just what sort of proposition might that be?"

"Take me to where my father is. You'll be well paid when we get there, I promise you. If you get me there before my father dies, I'll—that is, he'll pay extra."

Drew nodded his head and looked down at the faded rag rug before looking at her again. "Am I to take it, then, that your father will pay me for escorting you to his bedside?"

"That is correct, Mr. Kingman. My father is a man of . . . some wealth."

"I see."

She could tell he didn't believe a word she'd said. She'd have to give him something else as an incentive. But what? She had nothing! She cast about for an idea, anything that might get him to consider her offer.

"Mr. Kingman, it's true that my father left our family when I was five years old, but that does not mean that he forgot about us entirely. On the contrary. In fact, my father—"

"I'll do it."

"—sent us money regularly, and—What did you say?"

"I said, I'll do it."

Kate's thoughts dried up as effectively as water spilled in the dirt. "I don't understand."

"Frankly, ma'am, neither do I, but I'm heading generally that direction, and I don't see why I can't help you get to where your father is. Just where in Colorado does he live?"

If she told him the truth, she might not be able to trust him, so she lied again, wishing all the while that she didn't have to.

"Denver." She had no idea whatsoever if Denver was anywhere close to Silverton, but she figured it had to be since they were both in Colorado. It would do until she had to reveal the truth—after they were on their way.

Drew looked at her a long time. "Denver." He nodded.

She averted her eyes again, squirmed on the cushion, and straightened her skirts even though they lay perfectly smooth across her knees. "Well, Mr. Kingman, when can we get started? Time is of the essence, as you have been quite right to remind me."

"I was planning to leave Laramie this morning, ma'am, but we can wait until tomorrow if you need to . . . well . . . if there's anything you have to take care of. Denver's not that far."

"There's nothing, Mr. Kingman. I'll pack my belongings and be ready within the hour." Not that far? Ben had said that Silverton was almost to New Mexico. Colorado must not be as large a state as Kate had pictured it.

"I'll get the horses and come back here for you in an hour, then." Drew stood up and started to leave, then stopped and turned back. "If it's all right with you, ma'am, I'll see if I can trade your brother's horse for a good pack mule to carry our food and supplies."

She nodded and tried to swallow the lump that formed in her throat at the mention of her brother.

Drew replaced his hat and left the hotel.

An hour later, Kate came down stairs and stood by the front door. She had the telegram carefully folded and stuffed into her right boot.

Meg came out of the kitchen and handed her a small bundle. "Some cornbread and roast beef. For when you get hungry."

"Thanks, Meg." Kate hated to leave this place. Meg had been so wonderful to her.

Meg handed Kate the sacque coat she'd worn the night before. "You'll need this in those mountains, child." Meg ran her hands lovingly over the coat. "It gets powerful cold after the sun goes down." She dabbed at her eyes, then handed the sacque and another bundle to Kate. "You might as well have her dresses, too. God bless ya, child." Meg's eyes shone with tears.

"Thank you, Meg." Kate hugged the woman and shed a few tears of her own. "I'll never forget your kindness to me. And I'll treasure the dresses—and your daughter's memory."

"If you're ever up Laramie way again, you come by now, hear?"

"I hear."

Drew appeared at the door. He cleared his throat and waited until the ladies had composed themselves. "Are you ready, Miss Mathison?"

"I'm ready, Mr. Kingman."

Meg gave back some of the money Drew had paid for Kate's room and board for the whole week, then they left the warmth and security of the hotel. Meg stood on the front porch and waved. "You be careful, now!"

"Bye, Meg." Leaving made Kate feel empty inside and utterly alone again, but then she reminded herself she wasn't alone. Drew Kingman would stay with her until she found her pa in Silverton. With a timid smile and a shuddering deep breath, she promised herself she'd never be completely alone again, and hoped it wouldn't prove to be another lie.

Drew straightened the reins leading the mule he'd loaded with supplies. "Let's move out."

"I'm ready when you are." Kate clucked her tongue at the horse and headed down the street. Kate knew she'd made either the best decision of her life or the worst. She sincerely hoped it wouldn't turn out to be the latter.

When the sun reached its peak at noon in the cloudy sky, Drew reined in his horse. "We'll stop here."

"I'm perfectly capable of going on, if that's what you would normally do when traveling alone." Kate felt weary and dog-tired already, but she was determined not to let it show if she could help it.

"The horses need about an hour to rest and graze before we go on."

"Of course." Ben had always stopped for an hour about lunchtime, but Kate thought he'd done it to let her rest. She stepped to the ground from the horse. Straightening took a couple of minutes, then she had to get her legs working right again. Having to twist her ankles into the stirrups had made her back and legs ache terribly. Riding a sidesaddle probably would have been worse, though, with the way it bent a woman's knees around that ridiculous horn. Still, she wished she had one, just for looks. So far, Drew hadn't said anything about her riding astride. For that matter, he hadn't said much about anything else, either.

"Would you care for some water?" Drew offered his canteen.

"Thank you. I would." She drank more of the cool water

than she really should have, then handed it back.

Drew took a long pull, too, then hung the canteen back on his saddle. "We'll be in Colorado before long."

Colorado. Finally! It seemed ages since she and Ben had left Montana. "You said you were from Texas, Mr. Kingman. Is that where you were born?"

"Yep. About fifty miles from where my cattle ranch is—or was." He fished in the pack for a minute, then sat down next to a smooth rock and handed her a piece of beef jerky. He pushed his hat to the back of his head, leaned back, and bit off a chunk from another piece he'd gotten for himself.

"Was? What happened to it?" She worried a piece of the leathery meat from the chunk and chewed slowly.

"The ranch is still there. Just no cattle."

It wasn't any of her business, but he'd aroused her curiosity. "What happened to them?"

"Hoof and mouth disease, mostly. And rustlers."

"That's mighty poor luck, Mr. Kingman." Kate remembered when he'd said those words to her. "I'm sorry."

"I've been tracking the rustlers for weeks. I hoped to catch them before they sold my beeves, but I was too late."

"You never found the men who stole your cattle?"

"Just one of them." He didn't look at all pleased about it. "In Sutterfield."

They took another drink of water to get rid of the salty taste, and then Drew pulled his hat down over his eyes and leaned back against a rock. "Grab a nap if you're tired," he said, and went directly to sleep.

It amazed Kate that he could go to sleep whenever he chose to do so. Listening to his snoring made her drowsy, too, even though she'd slept quite well the night before. She was about to nod off when a memory struck her like lightning. He'd caught up to one of the rustlers—in Sutterfield. The scene played through her mind while fear crept through her . . .

After reading the telegram from Pa, Kate ran toward home—right past the saloon. The tinny sounds of the out-of-tune piano abruptly ceased, replaced by shouts, gunshots, and the unmistakable noise of a brawl. Kate veered off the board sidewalk, heading across the street to avoid the ruckus, but not soon enough to miss seeing two men, followed by a third, running for their lives out the swinging doors of the saloon.

"Get the sheriff! There's been a killin'!" the first man hollered.

"Never mind the sheriff! Let's get outta here before we're next!" The second man shoved past the first, grabbed his horse's reins, swung into the saddle, then kicked hard and went galloping down the street. The second man followed, leaving the third man standing on the sidewalk, his face red with anger.

With a shudder that had nothing to do with the chill night air, Kate realized the angry man in Sutterfield at the saloon was the man lying on the ground, just across the campfire from her. Drew Kingman.

What had she done?

Drew shook her shoulder about an hour later and woke her. When she saw him looking down at her, she cried out and pushed away. Seeing him silhouetted against the sun, just as she had when he'd pointed his gun at her—at the snake—made her stomach roil with fear.

"Whoa, there. You must've been having a bad dream. You're safe, I promise."

Kate reminded herself of where she was, and that she shouldn't let on that she knew who he was—or what he'd done in Sutterfield. "I'm sorry. I guess you're right. I must have been dreaming. You startled me."

"We'd best be getting on, ma'am. I'd like to make a few miles before we stop for the night." Drew reached for his horse's reins and the mule's lead. Kate blinked a few times, stretched, and pulled herself up off the ground. The nap had refreshed her more than she'd expected. She'd need to be rested so she could figure out what to do.

They rode on in silence. After another hour had gone by, Kate winced at the pain in her ankles and knees and took her feet out of the stirrups from time to time to ease the strain. If her legs didn't get used to riding soon, she might not be able to walk straight. If Drew Kingman had killed that man in Sutterfield, then her life might also be in danger. Somehow, it didn't add up, though. Drew didn't seem like a man who would gun someone down for no reason. If the man he killed had stolen his cattle, then he might have been entirely justified in killing him.

She decided to wait and see what happened next. Right now, her options were limited to the decision she'd made in Laramie. Only a low-down rotten scoundrel would harm a woman he'd promised to protect.

When Drew finally decided to make camp for the night, Kate felt proud that she'd kept up with the pace he'd set. She and Ben hadn't traveled this fast, and she felt more confident that she'd reach Silverton in time after all, and that she'd chosen well when she asked Drew Kingman to escort her. Just because he followed those two men out of the saloon didn't mean he'd killed anyone. In fact, the man who'd been killed might have been Drew's friend, and the two might have been the rustlers. That would certainly account for his anger. But, he'd said he caught up with only one of the rustlers. It was easy to see she didn't have all the facts, but she wasn't about to ask him for the missing pieces.

Drew pulled a package of sourdough starter out of his pack and commenced to make biscuits while Kate gathered wood for a campfire. Later on, the aroma of the biscuits, baking in a

Dutch oven, made her mouth water. Kate heated some beans to go with them, and when they sat down to eat and dipped the crunchy biscuits in the bean juice, Kate thought it had to be one of the best camp meals she'd ever eaten.

After the plates and cups were scrubbed clean, Drew settled down by the fire and stared into the flames.

Distant peaks swallowed the lowering sun, and shadows crawled across the land until darkness nestled around them. The only light came from the fire and from the winking stars scattered above them. The night sounds whispered and called to them, while the breeze, fragrant with sage, caressed their faces. Kate took a long, deep breath and studied Drew whenever he wasn't looking.

He was handsome, to say the least, but the reason, she decided, was the strength in his features. His square jaw, his nose—straight but not too big—and his gentle eyes gave Drew Kingman a look of importance. She'd seen him gussied up in a nice suit of clothes, and could almost picture him as a duke or a count or some other hoity-toity bigwig. The silly idea made her want to laugh until she remembered the anger in his eyes at the saloon.

Right now, he was leaning back against a rock with a blade of sweet grass between his teeth. He'd crossed his ankles and pulled his hat down over his eyes to shade them from—Well, she didn't know what his hat was shading him from, unless it was the light from the fire, and that didn't make much sense. He'd been a rancher, all right, yet there was more to Drew Kingman than first met the eye. Kate wished she could find out more about this man who'd nervously asked her to supper after saving her from a rattlesnake.

"What are you looking at?" Drew asked suddenly. "Do I have something between my teeth again?" He gave them a quick scrub with his sleeve.

"No! Nothing. I wasn't looking at anything." She got up and busied herself with her blanket and scolded herself for letting him catch her browsing. She'd have to be more careful about where she let her gaze get stuck.

After the fire died a bit and the night chill settled in, Kate wrapped herself in her blanket. Drew was already snoring softly. It took Kate a long time to get to sleep.

The next morning, Drew noticed the riders first, about an hour out of camp. "See there? Three of them. No, four."

"Who are they?" Kate squinted against the sun, but the riders appeared only as specks on a horizon of low pines and scrub brush. She also got the impression of a white hat and maybe a red shirt.

"Don't know." He glanced at Kate. "Don't want to know. Maybe they won't spot us."

He seemed nervous and Kate wondered why. It was normal to be wary of strangers in this wild, unsettled land, but Drew's concern seemed to be more than that. The riders disappeared after a spell and Drew relaxed a bit. He didn't mention them again.

Making camp that evening, Drew took care of the horses while Kate gathered wood for their campfire. She and Drew already had settled into a routine of sharing chores, and each knew just what to do. But Kate missed the conversations she'd shared with Ben. They'd talked about everything on the trail, and in the evenings, Ben entertained her with his harmonica while she sang along on the old songs they'd known all their lives. The songs Ma had taught them when they were wee babies.

Drew hadn't said a handful of words since that night at the café. Kate was starved for words and songs, so after they finished supper and packed away the gear for the night, she decided to strike up a conversation. It didn't much matter what Drew said as long as he made some noise that wasn't a whinny, a snort, or a bray.

"Mr. Kingman?"

"Yes, Miss Mathison?"

"Tell me about Texas."

"Texas?"

"Tell me about your ranch."

"Not much to tell. No one there, now that I'm here."

"Did you live there alone?"

He frowned and pitched another stick on the fire. "For the past eighteen months, I did."

Kate knew she shouldn't pry, but she couldn't help herself. She needed words to feed her soul. "And before that?"

He reached for his blanket and saddlebags, mumbled something she didn't hear because of the hooting of an owl, and took longer than he should have returning to the fire.

"Pardon?"

"I said, before that I lived on the ranch with my wife."

"Oh. I see." The heat in her cheeks added to the heat of the fire on her face, and she knew she'd poked too far into his personal business.

"She died of smallpox, two years come December."

"I'm sorry."

"So am I."

Drew shook his blanket a couple of times, spread it on the ground, and stretched out on it. Last night, he'd rolled up in the blanket, rested his head on his saddlebags, and fallen asleep all in one motion. She suspected he intended to do the same now, but he surprised her.

"Ever been married?" Shadows cast by the flames hid part of his face.

"Can't say that I have." Kate was touchy about having reached the age of twenty-five without so much as a single beau, much less a proposal of marriage. Her future as an old maid was signed and sealed.

"You look like her," Drew said quietly.

Kate looked up sharply. "What? What did you say?"

"I said, you look like her. My wife." He stared at her for a long time. Then, without warning, he rolled up in the blanket and rested his head on the saddlebags. "Better get some sleep."

Kate pulled her blanket over her. So. She reminded him of his wife. His dear, departed wife. Maybe that had something to do with his decision to take her to Colorado. Well, whatever the reason, she was glad. She had no idea who else she might have persuaded to take her. Not just anyone could be trusted. And she wasn't all that certain that Drew Kingman could be trusted, either. She fell asleep listening to the crackling of the fire and the shrill chirping of a cricket calling his mate.

Just past midnight, Drew sat up straight and reached for his gun. "They're coming," he said quietly.

Kate heard the bite in his voice and sat up. "The riders?" She gathered the blanket around her as though it could somehow protect or hide her from the intruders.

"Yep. I'm going to check on the horses. You stay here."

He left her by the dying fire. "Are the horses all right?" she whispered when he returned.

"Fine. Have you heard anything else?"

"Nothing."

The sound of drumming hooves reached them from the darkness. Drew eased around the fire to where Kate sat hugging her knees, trying not to be afraid.

"Put some more wood on the fire." Drew's voice was barely audible.

She did as he said and the fire blazed higher. Somehow, having more light to see by made her feel a little better.

The snorting and blowing of the horses got louder until the

first of the riders appeared at the edge of the fire's light.

"Hello, the camp!" a man called, and got down from his horse.

Drew stood. "Come forward and share the fire!"

Wasn't it a mistake to be friendly to them? "But—"

"Quiet." Drew's hand lingered over his holster.

Another man appeared. Both tied their horses to a bush just beyond the circle of firelight, then approached the camp.

"Howdy," the first man said. His clothes were dirty, his boots old and worn, and his hat stained with sweat and grime from the trail. The second man looked the same, except for a fancy bowler hat with a red feather stuck in the band on the right side. The feather matched his red flannel shirt.

"Howdy," Drew said carefully. "You're traveling late. Come and sit a spell."

"Much obliged," the first man said. He glanced from Drew to Kate. "Ma'am." He tipped his hat. "I'm Seth Brumley. This here's Cole Springer."

"I'm Drew Kingman. This is my wife, Kate."

Kate nodded slightly but said nothing. The word "wife" echoed in her mind. She pulled the blanket tighter.

Brumley and Springer squatted and held their hands toward the fire. "There's a nip in the night air already." Brumley spat into the fire. The coals popped and sizzled.

"Where are you headed?" Drew never took his eyes off Brumley.

"Laramie."

"You're three days out."

"You and your missus headed north or south?" Springer asked.

"East." He bumped his shoulder against Kate's.

"East, huh?"

Kate smiled and nodded, scared to say a single word. Who

were these men? Did Drew know them?

"Well, I guess we'd best be moving on." Brumley stood and stretched his back. "I wouldn't want to impose any longer on your hospitality."

Drew hesitated, then said, "You're welcome to share the fire longer if you're of a mind to."

"That's right neighborly of you, but we'd best be moving north. A friend of mine lost a brother to a no-good thief. We aim to help track him down."

Drew said nothing. Kate tried not to shake with fear when she felt Drew's arm tighten around her shoulders.

Brumley nodded and tipped his hat toward Kate, muttered, "Ma'am," then he and Springer disappeared into the darkness.

Kate sat as stiff as a ramrod until she heard their horses snort and whinny and hooves pounding the ground. She slumped and breathed a shuddering sigh of relief.

Drew blew out a long breath. "I'm sorry, Kate, but I thought it best to let them think—"

"No need to apologize. I appreciated what you did more than you could ever know." Kate held one hand over her eyes for a moment and scolded herself for feeling the need to cry. When she looked up again, he was smiling. His expression caught her entirely by surprise. "What is it?"

"I do believe that's the first time I've used your given name, except to tell Mrs. McGruder who you were."

"I believe you're right." Kate felt self-conscious and nervous and scolded herself for such feelings. Just because he'd called her Kate . . .

"I hope you understand what I'm about to say, Miss Mathison. I think we ought to sleep near one another tonight."

Kate felt her cheeks burn again. "Why is that?"

"Only two men came to the fire. There were four riders before."

"Are you sure they were the same men you saw earlier?"

"Reasonably. Springer was wearing a red shirt. There's a fair chance they didn't visit our fire just to warm their hands."

"I don't understand." Kate felt cold suddenly, and shivered.

"I don't trust them. Riding up in the middle of the night, stopping to sit by the fire a few minutes, telling us their private business—it doesn't wash."

"What do you suspect they're up to?"

He hesitated. "For safety's sake, I think we ought to stick close tonight, in case they come back. If they saw us sleeping apart after being told we were married—"

She shivered again. "I see your point entirely. You're absolutely right." Kate lay down again and rolled up in the blanket. She tried to calm herself while Drew banked the fire, picked up his blanket and came to where she lay. He eased down beside her as carefully as if he were lying down on a bed of eggs, and even after he stretched out, she could tell he hadn't relaxed. He was so close, she could hear him breathing.

The cold settled and penetrated all the way to her bones, even through the heavy sacque and the blanket. Her teeth chattered.

"Mr. Kingman?" she whispered, thinking he might already be asleep.

"Yes, Miss Mathison?"

"Are you c-cold?"

"No. Are you?"

"F-freezing."

Drew got up and pitched a few more sticks on the fire while she turned to face the flames. He settled on the other side of her. It helped some, but she still couldn't stop shivering.

"Miss Mathison?"

"Y-yes?"

"Begging your pardon and all, ma'am, but if I were to pull

you close beside me, we'd both stay warmer."

Kate swallowed hard. "I th-think that's a v-very practical s-suggestion."

Drew eased next to her. The blankets bunched between them. This time, Kate could feel the rise of his chest against her back with every breath he took.

"Begging your pardon again, ma'am, but if we were to use your coat as padding against this cold ground and spread the two blankets over both of us . . ."

"I s-see your point. Very well." Kate spread the coat beneath them, then held her breath while he spread the blankets carefully over the two of them. By this time, she was shaking all over, with cold and a fierce case of the jitters.

Being as careful as if he were handling live coals from the fire, Drew slipped his arm around her waist and pulled her next to him. His warmth seeped through her back, and she eventually stopped shivering.

"Are you warmer now?"

"Quite so. Thank you."

Kate realized she'd begun to breathe in rhythm with Drew. The realization embarrassed her, somehow. It seemed almost intimate. She pushed the feelings aside and tried to think about sleep instead. The warmth from his body soothed and relaxed her. She knew she should go to sleep, but with his arm around her middle . . ."

"Mr. Kingman?"

"Yes, Miss Mathison?"

"It has occurred to me, if those men come back, it would be terribly suspicious if we called each other by our surnames instead of our given names."

"You're right about that."

"In that case, you may call me Kate."

"Call me Drew."

Kate took several breaths along with Drew and tried not to gasp whenever his arm tightened or moved a little.

"Good night, Drew."

"Good night, Kate.

CHAPTER FIVE

When Kate opened her eyes the next morning, she was alone under the blankets. Trying to hold her eyes open was a chore, so she lay with them closed for a little longer, letting her body come back to life gradually before she faced the dazzling morning sun. She heard footsteps and sat up quickly.

"It's just me," Drew told her with a smile. "Don't get up unless you want to."

"We have to be on our way," she muttered, and tried to gather her wits about her. She folded the blankets and rolled them up, then joined Drew at the fire.

"Coffee?" He offered a cup that steamed in the morning chill.

"Please." She took the hot tin cup from him, using her skirt to protect her hands. She sipped the near-boiling coffee slowly and carefully and felt the warmth trickle through her by inches.

Drew pulled a small pan from his saddlebags and placed something carefully inside, then held out the pan for her to see.

"Eggs! Where on earth did you find them?" Kate's mouth watered at the sight of the brown speckled delicacies.

"Prairie chickens. I saw a pair of them when I got up and decided to nose around a bit. I got lucky." He splashed some water from the canteen over the four eggs and held the pan over the fire. "We don't have much to go with them, but—"

"It doesn't matter. It's been so long since I had a fresh egg, I couldn't begin to tell you how glad I am to see them." Kate smiled and found that she admired the way his eyes crinkled at the corners when he smiled back.

"Sleep well?" He glanced at her then back at the eggs.

"Better than I've slept in weeks. I . . . I guess it was because I was completely warm for the first time in days."

"Probably so." He busied himself with the pan.

Feeling self-conscious, she looked away, and he did, too.

"How long before those eggs will be done?"

"Not long. We'll need the plates and the forks from that bag over there."

"I'll get them." Kate hopped up, feeling like a new person. Maybe having those rough-looking characters wander into their camp had been a blessing in disguise. Tonight, though, there wouldn't be any threat. Or, at least, she hoped there wouldn't be. Would Drew suggest they double up on sleeping again? If he did, what should she say?

"They should be just about ready." Drew shook the pan a little and drained the water.

Kate hurried back with the plates and forks. Her mouth watered from the sight of the eggs being cracked. The whites were cooked just right while the dark yellow yolks stayed runny, just the way she liked them.

They said little until the four eggs were gone and the plates wiped clean with a couple of the leftover biscuits from two nights ago.

"Mighty good breakfast, Miss Mathison." Drew reached for another cup of coffee.

"You're supposed to call me Kate, remember?" she said carefully. "In case those men decide to come back."

"I plumb forgot. Kate. That's a mighty pretty name, too. I'll try not to forget again."

"See that you don't—Drew." The name felt good just saying it. Why did she feel so—well—so close to him this morning?

Maybe it was because he seemed friendlier somehow. She'd think about it later, though. The sun climbed higher into the sky by the minute and they had miles and miles yet to go.

Kate scrubbed the plates clean with some sand and tucked them back into the pack, along with the forks. "How long do you think it's going to take us to get to Silverton?"

"Silverton? I thought you said Denver." His eyes narrowed.

Kate ducked her head and scolded herself for carelessness. "I told you Denver because it's near Silverton, and I thought you might not have heard of such a small town in the mountains," she said lamely, avoiding his eyes.

"Everyone's heard of Silverton, Kate."

"Good! Then you know exactly how to get us there." She busied herself with tidying up the camp and getting everything packed on the horses, and tried to ignore her mistake.

"There's only one problem," he said quietly.

"Oh? What's that?"

"Silverton is on the other side of the Rocky Mountains from Denver. I wish you'd told me a little sooner."

"The other side? Why, they're both in Colorado, aren't they?" Her cheeks started to burn again. What a mistake! How could she have been so stupid?

"Yes, Kate, they're both in Colorado, but the Rockies run right down the middle of the state. We'll have to backtrack some if Silverton is really where we're going. Or are you going to change your mind again in a couple of days and decide that it's Oregon where your pa is dying?"

Kate held her chin a little higher and tried to hide her embarrassment. He wouldn't have been so flippant about her father if he believed her story. She'd just have to convince him all over again.

"Silverton is where my father is, Mr. Kingman. I have it right here in the wire he sent." She reached into her boot and pulled out the yellow paper, but didn't show it to Drew. She couldn't let him see the part about the silver. She looked at the message briefly, then refolded it and stuck it back into her boot. "Do you know the way to Silverton?" Her knees shook like aspen leaves in the fall.

Drew took off his hat and scratched his head. "Yes, Miss Mathison, I know the way." He put his hat back on and pulled the brim down low in the front. "All right, then. Silverton it is. I wish you'd chosen a town on the west side of the Rockies when you decided to lie about where it is I'm taking you. We'd have a lot shorter trip ahead of us." He made her feel like a wayward child.

She looked away, ashamed. From now on, she knew she'd better tell the truth! She shuddered to think about what he'd say when he learned that her pa wasn't on his deathbed.

"Ready?" A tightness in his lips made the word sound flat.

"Drew, I'm sorry, I truly am. I never meant to mislead you so dreadfully. I just—"

"Nothing to be sorry about, Miss Mathison. I'm just wondering if you have any more little surprises tucked away in your boots."

Kate gulped. Did she dare tell him the rest? He might not take her on to Silverton if he knew she was going for the money and not out of love for her cantankerous old rat of a father. When they got to Silverton, she'd tell him. Not before.

"Nothing else, Mr. Kingman." They were back to surnames again.

"Let's get moving, then." He stepped up into his saddle.

Kate pulled herself up onto the horse and fussed with the reins, thinking she should be used to riding after all these days on horseback, but her legs simply hadn't made up their minds to adjust to the situation yet. Riding still pained her, and she suspected it would until they reached Silverton.

About three hours later, Drew reined in his horse. He listened and searched the terrain, then stiffened.

"Drew? What is it—"

"Quiet!"

Kate tried to see what he was looking at, but all she spotted was a blue jay in a blue spruce, squawking at a squirrel on a lower branch.

They'd been heading west and the going was harder now, rockier. Drew stood up in his stirrups and stretched, peering intently toward the north.

Kate came up alongside and waited to hear his reason for stopping. She took the opportunity to take her feet out of the stirrups and stretch her cramped muscles.

"Three riders. Come on. Get down and follow me." He led her to a clump of piñon pines next to an outcropping of sandstone, then handed the reins to her. "Stay here."

Kate nodded and hunkered down, wondering what or whom they were hiding from. The horses and the mule, glad for a break, lowered their heads to nibble at some weeds growing between the rocks. Kate watched while Drew crept around a boulder jutting from the outcropping, and eased up onto another huge rock, giving him a better view. He stayed gone only a couple of minutes.

"What's down there?" Kate felt the urge to whisper but thought it silly when she didn't even know what was going on.

"Three riders. Can't tell what they're up to. They could be the same bunch who visited our fire last night. They're still pretty far away."

"I thought Brumley said they were headed for Laramie."

"He did. If these are the same men, then Brumley is a liar."

The word hung between them. Kate felt her cheeks warming and tried not to care if Drew Kingman thought her a liar, too. She tried to concentrate on the riders instead of her reputation.

Drew motioned for her to follow, and they went back down the way they'd come, mounted, and headed east.

"Where are we going?" They'd adjusted their destination this morning, and now Drew had changed directions again.

"We're going to see if they're following us or just passing through."

For the rest of the afternoon and most of the next morning, Drew led them a wandering path that eventually curved west again.

Drew checked on the riders once an hour. "They're trailing us," he said after the third check.

"Are you sure?"

"Yep. And I think I recognized one of the riders. If it's who I think it is, we may be in for some trouble."

"Who is it?"

"Just do what I tell you and don't ask any questions. Got it?"

Kate opened her mouth to protest that she ought to at least know whom they were running from, but she knew it wouldn't do her a bit of good. So she nodded, angry to be ordered around. Yet Drew seemed to know what he was doing, and for that she was grateful.

They stopped at noon to eat, then rode in silence the rest of the afternoon, trying not to call any attention to themselves. Every hour or so, Drew climbed a boulder or a hill and studied the group of men who dogged their tracks. By the time Drew decided to stop to camp for the night, Kate was exhausted. More than anything, she longed for a hot bath and a soft bed and the chance to yell if she felt like it, which she did. What would happen, she wondered, if she were to cut loose with a hair-raising scream? Drew bumped her elbow and she almost did!

"We'll have to keep our fire low again tonight." Drew's eyes were narrow, his forehead lined.

"Why?"

Drew stared at her as though she were completely daft. "So they won't know where we are."

"Are they aware that we know they're following us?"

"I reckon they are."

"If we build our fire big, just like we didn't know they were there, wouldn't that give us an edge if they decide to jump us tonight? I mean, if they didn't know we were expecting them . . ."

Drew thought it over. "All right, let's try it your way. Oh, and by the way, I was right. Jerome Carson is one of them. And Brumley and Springer are with him."

"Then Brumley and Springer—Who in tarnation is Jerome Carson?"

"The brother of the rustler I tracked out of Kansas."

"So?"

"So, when Tom Carson tried to kill me, I had to shoot him. Carson thinks I killed his brother in cold blood and stole his money."

"But it was your money."

"I know that, and you know that, but Carson doesn't. I doubt if he'll let me explain before he blows my head off."

Kate paled. "Let's build this fire as big as we can build it, Drew. Then we'll hide in the dark. When they come in—"

Drew held up one hand to silence her. "They may not wait till dark. In fact, I'm surprised they've waited this long. Get down."

Kate dropped to her knees. Drew eased over to a high spot and peered into the draw below. Dusk had deepened the foothills to shades of gray, making it harder to pick out one object from another in the shadows.

"They've stopped for the night." He spoke in a hushed voice. "Gather some wood. Your idea sounds as good as any I've heard yet."

Kate squinted and tried to spot the men making camp, but everything lay in deep shadow. How could Drew see in such dim light? With a sigh, she went to gather wood.

The stars blinked on, one by one. Drew had built the fire normal size. He and Kate warmed themselves but made no move to cook or even boil a pot of coffee.

"Kate, get on your horse."

"Now? Why?"

"We're going to move on down the valley and let Carson and his bunch think we're still right here. By the time they know we're not . . ."

Kate nodded. She knew her horse must be as weary as she was from their long day's ride, but hopefully they'd rest soon. They had to, or she wouldn't be able to sit a saddle tomorrow.

Two hours later they stopped for the night. Drew found a spot surrounded by rocks and pines that would protect them from the wind and hide their second, smaller campfire from Jerome Carson and his men. The new place also gave Drew the advantage of height if they were found.

They ate in silence, then Kate reached for her blanket.

"Doubling up worked pretty good before." Drew's voice was low and gruff.

"Sure did." Kate held her breath.

"Want to try it again tonight? It's liable to be a good bit colder, now that we're higher. And we can't build up the fire."

"Sounds good to me," Kate said nervously. She was actually looking forward to having Drew's arm around her again. Never had a man held her close, not even Ben, and she'd long ago resigned herself to being a maiden lady for the rest of her life. Having a strong arm around her was something she'd never expected to experience. Lying next to Drew for the sake of warmth and protection was the smart thing to do. Pleasant and exciting, too.

Drew gave her the warmer place, next to the fire, and waited until she had settled next to him before he pulled the blankets over them and eased his arm around her.

"Is my arm too heavy, Kate?"

"No, it isn't."

"If it gets too heavy, you just tell me."

"I shall."

They lay there, perfectly quiet. The night sounds seemed louder around them—the croak of a tree frog, the call of an owl, the whisper of the mountain wind through the pines. This was different country from what Kate was used to. Sutterfield squatted among broad grasslands, with no mountains anywhere in sight. Now that they were coming into the edge of the Rockies, Kate felt almost cradled by the distant foggy peaks. And the rolling hills, a hint of the majestic mountains yet to come, sheltered them as no grass-covered plain could ever do.

Kate listened to Drew's breathing, deep and rhythmical, and decided he must be asleep. Carefully, so she wouldn't disturb him, she rolled onto her back and surveyed the dazzling display above them. Thousands of stars twinkled in the moonless sky. Kate thought of a bolt of indigo velvet she'd admired in a store in Sutterfield, and remembered how she'd longed to have a dress made from it. Someday, she'd have a dress like that. Since Pa had found the silver, she'd be able to buy velvet in any color she wanted—even pink! The skirt would drape in luscious folds. She might even scatter sequins or pearls over an indigo dress so it would have the same sparkling appearance as the sky, peppered with stars.

Drew took in a sharp breath, resulting in a snort that almost made Kate laugh out loud. Ben had snored, but never so loudly that he'd kept Kate awake. Drew didn't start snoring, though. After that one snort, his rhythmical breathing resumed. He'd shifted his position and his hand had moved from her waist to just below her left breast. If he were to shift again and actually touch her breast, would she be obliged to wake him? Or would it be best to wait until he shifted position again? What would it feel like to have him touch her in such an intimate way? He'd been married. The thought that he might be used to reaching for soft, feminine curves in the night made her feverish. Kate got warmer by the minute, in spite of the night air, chilled now that the fire was dying.

Kate decided maybe she ought to be the one to change position instead of waiting for him to do it on his own, so she pivoted onto her left side, away from him. The movement roused him just enough to make him move his arm again.

With a gasp, Kate felt his hand close over her left breast. She froze. What should she do now? His fingers tightened. She tried to swallow but couldn't. Slowly, gently, he caressed her, squeezing, stroking, finding every curve with his fingers until she thought she'd die with the exquisite pleasure. And it wasn't only her breast that felt queasy and warm. Her stomach tensed with each movement, and lower . . . she felt . . . what she'd never . . . felt . . . oh, my gosh . . . before . . .

Afraid it would stop—hoping it wouldn't—Kate closed her eyes tightly and sighed with disappointment when Drew removed his hand. And found her other breast. Every sensation doubled, trebled, as he gave it equal attention.

Kate knew she shouldn't let it continue, but she couldn't bring herself to wake him. If he knew what he was doing, it would make things exceedingly difficult between them. And she'd be ashamed for him to know that she'd allowed it to happen at all. No, the best thing to do was nothing. Eventually— oh, dear Lord, but it felt good—he'd roll over or shift position again, and no one would ever know what had happened. No one but her.

He pulled her closer and nestled into the soft curve of her

shoulder. His fingers continued to knead and stroke, and she made a little sound that came from her throat unbidden. He stopped cold and didn't move a muscle for almost a minute.

Was he awake? If so, should she push him away? Scream at him? Protest the liberties that he had taken with her while he slept? But she couldn't make herself move. And she didn't scream. Instead, she made that little noise again when his fingers tensed, then relaxed, and his thumb wandered over the soft curves pushing against the serge dress. She called his name, silently, not even a whisper.

Kate knew he was awake now. She'd felt him tense and still she could not make herself move. When he resumed his caresses, tears came to her eyes. She loved the feel of his hand where no man had ever touched before. Instead of pushing him away, she wished the dress would vanish. She wanted to know what that hand would feel like on her bare skin. She knew her thoughts were evil, yet she couldn't deny them. "Drew," she sighed again. His fingers pressed and rubbed, sending ripples of pleasure through her.

Drew pulled her over on her back. She kept her eyes closed. Could he tell that she enjoyed having his hand on her breasts? Did the little noises tell him so?

If only she could reach for him, the way she wanted to do. She wondered what his lips would taste like, feel like against hers. Did he think her evil? A woman of ill repute like May Belle?

Drew stroked the hair away from her temples. She still kept her eyes closed. Her breathing had become shallow and uneven. How much longer should she let it go on?

Kate wished with all her heart that he would kiss her. She'd already compromised herself, so she might as well have more to remember as she grew older, spending her nights alone, a poor maiden lady with no man to warm her bed, to pleasure her with sweet caresses. Would she spend the rest of her life not knowing what it was to be kissed?

In a rush of impatience, she opened her eyes. He was only inches away. His eyes were open and trained on hers. His fingers trailed over her cheek, touched her lips. Kate decided, then and there, she'd waited long enough. She twined her fingers through the hair on the nape of his neck. It felt soft, not coarse in the sensitive palm of her hand.

Drew's mouth hovered only an inch from her lips. Slowly, hesitantly, he pressed his mouth against hers. She didn't pull away or protest. He pulled her top lip into his mouth and she trembled. Her fingers at the back of his neck tensed, then slid up over his scalp, and she felt a shudder go through him.

His lips lay soft on hers, so soft. Never had her dreams been like this. When he ran his tongue around her lips, between them, Kate pulled him closer. He moved his hand from one breast to the other between them, teasing, rubbing, squeezing, holding, and the material of her dress strained more than usual from the push of her breasts against the buttons in the front.

He parted her lips then, and his tongue, velvety and alive, touched hers. All reason left her. Never had she imagined such pleasure. Never had she felt the heat of desire as she felt it now.

Kate felt his body, lean and strong, against her breasts, her stomach, her thighs. Even though she could not imagine herself ever allowing it, she longed to feel his bare skin against hers. Was his chest covered with hair the same color as that on his head? Was it as soft? Did it curl and stand out or was it straight, clinging to his skin? Would his stomach be flat and muscular, or would it be soft and showing the beginning of a paunch?

His fingers drove her crazy. His tongue in her mouth probed tenderly. The weight of him felt comfortable and warm. She let her hands wander up and down his back and over his shoulders and thanked the stars above that dreams did occasionally come true.

Drew leaned back just a bit and she opened her eyes.

"Kate?"

Not wanting to spoil fantasy with the reality of words, Kate pulled him down to kiss her again and he abandoned his caution and intensified the kiss. He worked his arms under her, then rolled over onto his back, bringing her with him. Now she was on top and free of his weight, free to do as she would with him.

Kate kissed him with passion and intense need, and Drew held her, stroked her back and shoulders, framed her face with his hands while he probed her mouth. She wanted love, warmth, and affection from him. But she had to stop. She had to. But oh, God, she didn't want to.

He rolled her over again then leaned back. She sensed his hesitance. She could tell by the tension in his shoulders and arms. Why? Didn't he want to kiss her anymore? Wasn't she pretty enough? Did her inexperience show so much?

Alone. He was leaving her alone. Thoughts of Ben crowded in and clawed at her, until, with a shudder, she let out all the fear and hurt and gave in to the grief, just as she had at the hotel. The tears came, and her shoulders shook until she had to turn away.

"Kate. Kate." Drew hugged her tighter. He held her until the pain eased, until she could be quiet in his arms. "Sleep now." He kissed her again, lightly this time.

Kate nodded and turned her back to him, just as they'd begun the night. Shame overwhelmed her, just as the feelings that refused to go away still overwhelmed her. And yet there was peace, too. And something she'd never felt before.

Drew pulled the blankets over them, just as he had an hour ago, and eased his arm around her.

"Good night, Drew."
"Good night, Kate."

CHAPTER SIX

The next morning, Kate roused when Drew eased out from under the blankets just before dawn, but she pretended to be asleep so she could watch him without having to say anything. Drew peered over the rocks, staying hidden from view, and scanned the terrain below, apparently searching for signs of Jerome Carson and his men. Judging from his lack of reaction, she decided there must be no sign of them. Drew looked back at Kate and almost caught her with her eyes open.

Then, something—a noise?—pulled him back to scrutinize the trees below. He tensed from head to foot, eased back down from the rock, being careful not to make a sound, and crept back to the camp.

"Kate, wake up."

"What?" She didn't know how he'd feel about being watched, so she pretended to awaken from a deep sleep.

"Keep your voice down. We have to get out of here. Now."

Kate heard the urgency in his voice and sat up. Her first look into Drew's eyes made her blush. The memory of what had happened the night before blazed crystal clear in her mind, but Drew gave all his attention to what he'd seen. She obeyed without another word.

"They're below us about a mile to the north," he said quietly. "We'll have to skirt this ridge and put some distance between us. It didn't take Carson long to figure out he'd been tricked."

Kate nodded and reached for her saddle, but Drew took it

from her. Their fingers touched for an instant. Kate took a deep breath and looked away. Within a couple of minutes, Drew had the horses saddled and their gear packed on the mule.

Kate stepped up into the saddle and waited for Drew to lead the way. They picked their way through the scrub pines, around boulders, and through a little pass leading down to a grassy meadow between the hills. Kate thought it would be a perfectly wonderful place for a cabin, but under the present circumstances, it was only coverless ground, where they could be spotted easily. Drew chose to follow the pines edging the meadow, and Kate followed as quietly as possible.

Once they reached the far side of the meadow, the terrain became rocky again, and the horses had a hard time with the steep incline. Their puffing and blowing echoed like gunshots through the stillness of the crisp morning.

"Just over this ridge the going should be easier." Drew directed his words to her with cupped hands, so his voice wouldn't carry.

Kate nodded. In spite of the peril they were in, she was thankful the day had begun this way. Eating breakfast, loading the horses in a casual, unhurried way, would have left time for talk, and Kate had no idea what she was going to say to Drew once the tension eased. And what on earth were they going to do tonight, when the wind bit colder and they'd have to huddle together to stay warm? How could she lie next to him again and wonder if he'd keep his hands to himself? How could she lie so close to those sultry lips and not want them to touch her own?

A rustling behind them jarred her from the uncomfortable thoughts. "Drew!" she whispered urgently.

"What is it?"

"Back there. I heard something."

Drew stood up in the stirrups. Three riders came over the ridge they'd just crossed. One of them wore a red shirt. Kate's blood ran cold.

"Come on!" Drew kicked his horse into a trot. The trail made the going somewhat easier, but the grade continued to punish them as before. "We'll have to hide."

Drew looked around, searching for a likely place, then motioned for Kate to follow. Heading into the thickest part of the undergrowth, Drew fought the branches and briars out of his way.

"Drew! Where are we going?" A branch swung around and hit her squarely in the face. "Watch out!" she scolded him.

"Don't talk. Just come on!"

Kate struggled with the thick foliage, hoping she wouldn't be dragged from her horse. Finally, Drew stopped and got down.

"Over here." He motioned, and took her horse's reins when she dismounted. He led the three animals off to the left and disappeared behind a huge pine tree angling sharply from the side of the mountain.

"Drew! Don't leave me here!" Kate searched frantically in the dense undergrowth.

"Up here!" He stood above her on a ledge.

"How do I get there?"

"Come around the way I did. You'll see."

She did as he said, even though briars tore at her skirt and scratched her hands and face. Finally, she broke free and found where Drew had tied the horses and the mule. He'd climbed farther and waited on a ledge rimmed with saplings and briars.

"Give me your hand and I'll help you up. Hurry!"

The sound of approaching horses was louder than ever. Kate hitched up her skirts and tried to get past the poison ivy hanging from the trees, with no luck. The acrid rash showed up immediately on her left hand and tempted her to utter a few of the curse words she'd heard in the saloons back in Sutterfield.

"They're coming, woman!" He reached for her hand.

Stepping up on the rocks, Kate's shoes slipped. She let out a cry when Drew hoisted her up into his arms. There, only inches away from him, she gasped for breath and managed to say, "Thank you."

Drew stared into her eyes for a long moment before he turned her around and set her down on the ledge beside him. Tension circled them like something alive.

The crack of a broken stick reverberated through the stillness.

Drew pulled himself, flat on his belly, out to the lip of the ledge. Carson had stopped right below them. If he spied where they'd pushed through the brush, there'd be shooting and someone would die. Kate squeezed her eyes shut and tried not to gulp for air.

"We know you're here, Kingman." Carson's voice carried across the meadow and bounced off the western cliffs. "You killed my brother and I aim to kill you. Save us both some time and come out."

Kate gasped. Carson intended to kill Drew on sight!

Drew held one finger to his lips. Kate knew, if she made the slightest sound and gave away their position, she'd condemn Drew to death. Jerome Carson would never sit still to hear the truth about his no-good, cattle-thieving brother. He'd pull the trigger. For now, they had to grit their teeth and wait.

"There's no use trying to hide, Kingman. One way or another, I have to kill you." Carson motioned for his men to follow and headed across the meadow.

Drew waited until they were out of earshot, then pulled Kate close. "We'll have to backtrack."

"Backtrack? But, we'll never get to Silverton if we lose any more time. We've already lost two days because of Carson. Can't we just wait until they've gone?"

"Nope. It'll be only one more day, maybe two. By the time he knows to backtrack, our trail will be cold. He's been tracking me for better than ten days now. Pretty soon, he'll give up and go home."

"But you have no guarantee of that. What if he doesn't?"

"Then I'll have to find a way to get the truth to him, or—" He licked his lips. "I'll have to face him. I won't run like this much longer."

Kate knew, if she hadn't been with him, he wouldn't have run this long. She fought the tears. Seeing Drew in a gunfight against three men would be more than she could bear.

"Now, don't you worry none about getting to Silverton. You'll see your pa again, Kate. I promise."

He had misunderstood her tears, and she figured that might be best. She also knew he couldn't promise such a thing, but she appreciated the gesture anyway. Seeing her pa had to be the last thing on her mind right now, but if Drew stayed convinced they had to get to Silverton as soon as possible, it might save his life.

Once Drew was satisfied Carson had gone far enough not to hear them leave, they headed back the way they'd come but stayed in the shelter of the trees.

They reached the place where they'd spent the night a little past noon, gnawed on cold sourdough biscuits and salty beef jerky, and washed it down with cold stream water. Then they headed southeast, walking downstream for several miles, hoping to throw Carson completely off the track if he backtracked too soon. Even Carson couldn't track a horse down a running streambed.

The sun sagged lower in the sky. Kate, dog-tired, knew they had to put a few more miles behind them before they could stop. At the lower altitude, it would be warmer and double blankets might not be necessary. Kate had mixed emotions about that, but soon grew too tired to care one way or the other.

Her back ached to match her knees and ankles, and her head weighed so heavily on her neck and shoulders, she could hardly look straight ahead. Her chin bobbed in time with the horse's jolting gait as they rode on and on.

Kate cried with relief when Drew pulled up at dusk to make camp. They unloaded their gear within a clump of cedars beside a clean, gurgling stream. Kate scooped up a handful of the icy water and splashed it on her face and neck. Then she washed her hands and drank in thirsty gulps. The fresh water felt and tasted heavenly.

Drew seemed to be tired, too, but remained constantly on guard, alert to any sign that Carson might have figured out his trick, but there came no sign of him or the others from anywhere. Drew snared a rabbit, then relaxed by the fire and roasted it on a spit he'd made from a green branch. He kept the fire tight and smokeless.

The white, stringy rabbit meat tasted utterly delicious, and, washed down with clear water from the stream, Kate imagined it a dinner fit for royalty.

The night wind promised to be chilly, but nothing like the colder temperatures in the heights. Kate wished they had to sleep like spoons again to stay warm. The thought of Drew's hands on her body made her blush and filled unmentionable parts of her with longing. If he knew, would he suggest—

She wished it was colder than a Montana blizzard so he'd have to hold her tight against him again. Would he be a perfect gentleman this time, she wondered, and make his hands behave? Or would he touch and caress, thinking how smooth her skin must be beneath her dress, how tight her nipples grew when he brushed his knuckles across them. She wanted him to touch her again—without this tight dress. She wanted to feel his mouth against hers again, to have him kiss the slope of her long, slender neck, to—

She had to stop this! Right now!

"I think I'll turn in." Kate wished for a sudden icy wind to cool her fevered skin. The way he sat by the fire, with one leg bent flat and the other propped up, made her even more feverish.

"Good idea." He stared at her for a moment, then pitched another stick on the fire. "I'm going to stay up a while and keep watch."

His eyes fixed on her again and he did not look away this time. Could he be having similar thoughts?

She had to divert her mind again. "Should I take a turn later?"

"Maybe. If all's quiet, I'll catch a few winks later on." He looked away. Reluctantly? Into the deepening shadows.

"Whatever you say." Kate watched him longer than she should have, then reached for her blanket. "It isn't so cold tonight." She smiled nervously and tried not to stare at him again.

"We're lower. It won't be cold again until we're back in the heights." His eyes held hers again and he ran his tongue over his bottom lip, leaving it wet and glistening in the firelight.

"How long will that be?" Could she wait that long?

Drew poured another cup of strong coffee, then stared at her. Was he thinking the same thing she was thinking? Could it be he wanted it as much as she did? A lady like Kate shouldn't be thinking . . . He shifted positions and stretched his legs out in front of him. She let out a long breath.

"I said, how long will that be?" She decided he had the smoothest lips she'd ever seen on a man. Those lips against hers had felt like satin or silk. Or sinfully red velvet.

"About two days, I reckon," Drew said finally.

"Two days." How could she wait that long for him to touch her again? What would she do when—if—he did? His eyes lingered on hers again. Trailed down to her lips, her breasts, then slowly back up to her eyes.

Kate lay down on her coat and pulled the blanket around her shoulders. She found the blanket too heavy. Almost unnecessary. She turned it back, but the night air did nothing to cool the heat radiating from her. She couldn't look away from his face. His lips. His hands, so rough, yet so gentle. "Drew?"

He started to get up, then eased back down. "What is it, Kate?"

What, indeed? *Hold me. Kiss me. Touch me. Love me.* If she mentioned last night at all, it could—would—happen again. Last night had been an accident. There was no shame in something accidental, was there? If it happened again, though, it would be deliberate, and the last shreds of her dignity would be destroyed.

"Good night," she said weakly.

"Good night, Kate."

But she did not sleep.

Around midnight, he pulled his blanket around himself and lay very still. The fire had died and the chill had settled around them. It still wasn't cold enough for two blankets. *Too bad,* she thought.

His snores blended with the night sounds of crickets and frogs, and she slept.

They didn't see Carson the next day or the next, and by the third morning, Drew decided he'd given up.

"Can you be sure, though?" Kate folded her blanket carefully and helped to stash the supplies on the mule.

"No, but I'm pretty sure."

For the past three nights, they'd slept across the fire from each other. Neither had mentioned what had happened between them, and, because the nights had been warmer, neither had suggested doubling up for extra warmth. Tonight would be different, though. Tonight, they'd be back in higher country again, headed into the Rockies.

Drew packed his horse. "Ready?" he asked in his usual way.

"Ready." Their routine was firmly established by now, and Kate knew exactly which part she'd been given to play.

On the trail, Kate noticed a different smell in the air. The smell of winter. Even though November was still days away. The realization that they could be facing an early, unusually bad, winter made Kate nervous. She had a feeling, for the first time, they weren't going to make it to Silverton before the snows filled the mountain passes. Drew hadn't said a word about it, though, so maybe she was wrong. It couldn't hurt to ask him.

"Drew?"

He turned around in his saddle just enough to look at her. "What is it?"

She kicked her horse and pulled up beside him. "Are we going to make it to Silverton before snowfall?"

Drew looked into the distance ahead of them at the rugged peaks, some of which stayed snow-covered year round, and took a long, deep breath. "I doubt it." He looked back at her.

"Why are we going on, then?"

"Because I felt I had to try to get you there to see your pa, that's why." A trace of irritation colored his voice.

"But what will we do if we're caught in the snow?"

He didn't answer.

"Drew?"

"There's a cabin about twenty-five miles from here. By the time we reach it, we'll know whether or not we can go on. If we can, we will. If not, we'll have to turn back."

"Turn back! We can't turn back! Not now! I've come so far, I'm not about to take one step back unless I have to! Drew Kingman, you promised me you'd get me to Silverton and—"

"Whoa there, woman. Settle down!" He waited until she'd shut up. "I didn't say we had to turn back. I just didn't think you'd want to consider the alternative."

"Alternative? What, pray tell, might that be?"

He stared straight ahead. "To wait out the winter. Wait for the spring thaws, then go on to Silverton."

Kate shook her head to clear her thoughts. Was he talking about—

"The cabin!" he shouted. "We may have to spend the winter in the cabin!"

Kate's anger evaporated in the crisp morning air. "I see." Four months alone with him in a cabin. She gulped and released a sigh that clouded in front of her face. It was getting colder already. How could they ever expect to make Silverton before the first heavy snow? How could she live in a cabin with Drew Kingman, just the two of them, and not compromise every virtue she had and then some? She was strong, but not that strong!

Drew stared at the reins in his hand. "Or, we can turn back now."

Kate stuck out her lower lip, like a child.

Drew started to say something. Instead, he yanked hard on the reins and got down from his horse. "We'll stop here for a spell. I'll be back."

Kate got down from the horse and watched him go. He marched to a clump of junipers and stood there, muttering to himself. She decided to leave him alone.

Drew stared into the scraggly branches of the gray-green bush and cursed under his breath. She'd stuck out her bottom lip at him, just like a kid. Damn, but he wished he could kiss that lip, taste it, the way he had before. The way he'd been longing to do again for days now. Living with her in a cabin for the winter would be more than any man could be expected to endure. They had to turn back now. It was the only way to keep them both sane—and Kate's virtue intact.

"Drew?"

He turned around and saw her sitting on a rock, looking for all the world like a high-society female perched on a velvet cushion.

"What is it now?" he shouted at her, then realized she hadn't done or said anything to deserve being shouted at. His frustrations were beginning to get the better of him, and he had to do something about it soon, or . . . or . . . he didn't know what would happen.

"I'm sorry." Tears rolled down her cheeks.

"Sorry? There's nothing for you to be sorry for." He walked back toward her. "Don't you go bawling on me, now, you hear? I can't stand it when you cry, woman. So stop it! Stop it right now. Else I'm turning this horse around and heading right back to Laramie and you can freeze in the snow for all I care!" He was ranting and he knew it, taking everything out on her. But she was responsible, dammit! Even after all she'd been through, she deserved it!

Kate held her breath for a moment, then burst out in loud, soggy sobs.

God, but she was beautiful, even with her face wet and her eyes red.

He pulled her up from the rock and hugged her. "I'm sorry. Everything seems to be going wrong, and I don't know how to fix it. It isn't your fault Carson is tracking me and that dodging him cost us precious time. And it isn't your fault winter's decided to call early this year." *But it is your fault that you kiss like a whore in spite of the fact you've never been touched by a man in your life,* he told himself bitterly.

"There's no need to explain, Mr. Kingman. I am fully aware of why we aren't going to be able to reach Silverton in time."

Drew nodded a couple of times. "Mr. Kingman, is it, now?"

Kate swiped at her running nose with the back of one hand.

"And who was it the other night when you wanted to be kissed? Answer me that? Was that *Mister* Kingman? Who held you while you cried for your dead brother? And who touched you and held you and kissed you while you kissed right back? Answer me that! And who was it—who was it—" The look in Kate's eyes stopped him cold. Oh, God. What had he gone and said? "Kate, I didn't mean it—Kate!"

She spun around and pulled herself into the saddle, then kicked the horse's flanks hard. She had to get away from this man. The man who had shamed her. Who led her to shame herself. She had to get away before she begged him to shame her again.

The horse tried its best to keep up with the pace she wanted, but the terrain was too rough and rocky, and it soon became impossible.

Kate got down from the snorting, blowing animal and tried to run, but Drew cut her off. He stepped down from his horse and grabbed her by the shoulders.

"Leave me alone!" She flailed at him with her fists. "I hate you! I never want to see you again! Leave me alone! Leave me . . . leave me . . . alone!" Hiccups cut off her words and she collapsed against him, sobbing and hiccuping, feeling like a fool.

When Kate's sobs slacked off, she realized Drew was holding her, stroking her hair and her back, muttering something she hadn't been able to listen to.

"It's all right, Kate. It's all right. There's nothing to be ashamed of. It's all right."

Nothing to be ashamed of! If he thought she was the sort of woman who did such things without shame—!

Kate knew she should push him away, but she couldn't. No matter what he might think of her, no matter how shameful her behavior might be, she couldn't wait any longer. Drew held her tight against him and looked to the sky, wishing he could take back the words that had humiliated her so terribly. Only now did he realize what guilt she'd been lugging around since that night. By letting him touch and kiss her, she'd sacrificed her dignity and her pride, and the silence they'd maintained between them since that night had been the only way she could survive the shame she felt. But she'd done nothing wrong. Couldn't she see that? Needing someone in the middle of the night, when it was cold and dark, and feeling that everyone in the world who ever meant anything to you was either dead or dying—needing someone to care—there was nothing wrong with that, either.

Drew felt her tense up and he loosened his grip on her. When she looked into his eyes with that distraught expression that said she'd ruined herself by succumbing to her desire for him, he forgot all his promises, all his good intentions, and pressed his mouth to hers.

There, surrounded by towering peaks and shadowy valleys, Drew and Kate held each other the way they had that night. Only this time was different, because they were fully aware of what was happening, and the urgent heed to be closer was tenfold what it had been that night.

Drew pressed her tighter against him, reluctant to remove his mouth from hers for fear she'd never let him kiss or hold her like this again. Finally, though, he eased the pressure of the embrace, hoping she wouldn't run away and be ashamed all over again. She didn't.

Kate let his mouth go, regretting that she had to. She tilted her head back to study his expression and was startled to see anguish in his eyes. "Drew?"

"I'm sorry, Kate. I . . . I'm sorry."

"Sorry for what?"

"For what I said. I've . . . well, I've taken more from you than you were able to give. I'm sorry, that's all."

"You took nothing more than what I offered. If there's to be shame because of it, it's mine."

"No, don't you see?" He held her face with his hands. His breath steamed into the rapidly chilling air. "There's nothing for you to be ashamed of!"

"Do you honestly believe that?"

"Yes, I do. You've been through more than any woman should have to endure, and with no one to comfort and help you through it. Can't you see? There's no shame in being comforted when you're grieving."

"No, but—"

"Like it or not, Kate, I need you, too."

"You do?" The thought that Drew might need comforting had never occurred to her.

Drew looked away then, and pulled her head against his chest. Resting his chin above her forehead, he took a long shuddering breath.

"I married Lucy because I needed a wife and she needed a husband."

"You didn't love her?"

"I was fond of her. I needed someone to tend my house, and she'd lost her husband a few months earlier. It seemed the best thing for both of us. She was a good woman, but frail. We'd been married only a little over three months when she came down with smallpox. A drifter, so sick with the pox he couldn't walk straight, came through town and she happened to be in the general store the same time he was there. Lucy and the storekeeper died within two days of each other."

"How awful!"

"I buried her four months to the day after we were married."

"How terrible for you!" She pulled him closer.

"I didn't know how to feel, Kate. I was numb. I had to get

away." He stopped, unable to say more.

Kate saw him now with new understanding. "So, there was no one to comfort you, either."

"No one. Until now." He ran his fingers down the side of her face. "When I saw you the first time, you reminded me of her, though now I can't say why. You don't look like her at all. Not at all. That night when I touched you—" She stiffened in his arms. "I was thinking about Lucy before I fell asleep. I guess . . . I guess that's why I reached for you the way I did. I was reaching for her."

"But you woke up." She could scarcely breathe.

"Yes, I woke up, and when I realized what I'd done, I didn't know what to do to make it right. But you . . . you didn't turn away, and I couldn't figure out why. So, I accepted that you needed to be comforted the same as I did. And that's how it happened. We comforted each other." He took a long slow breath and seemed to be waiting to see what she'd say next.

Kate was too embarrassed to tell him the truth about why she hadn't stopped him, so she said nothing at all.

"I wish you wouldn't feel—"

"I don't anymore, Drew."

He tipped her chin upward until he was looking squarely into her eyes. "Are you sure?"

She smiled and nodded, feeling free from the burden of guilt that had weighed her down so miserably.

"So where do we go from here?"

"I don't know. You're the guide. You tell me." She meant it. For the first time since Ben's death, she was content to put her life and her destiny in someone else's hands. Not just anyone's hands, though. In Drew's hands. His most capable and tender hands.

"I think we have a chance to make it to Silverton," he said finally. "But, we're going to have to make good time if we're to keep that chance. What I said about us having to hole up in that cabin for the winter is still a possibility. Are you willing to do that if it's necessary?"

Kate knew now that she was. "Let's try to get there. I don't think I could stand it if we gave up now. We'll deal with whatever happens when it happens."

He nodded, loving the strength in her, and realized he wanted to kiss her again. Why not?

"Do you think we might comfort each other again?"

She came to him willingly, and the kiss was different, more sensitive, more arousing than any other kiss Drew could remember. Every time he kissed Kate, the rush of desire built in him until he felt he might burst. It came quicker, stronger, and took a lot longer to subside. Kissing her could get to be a habit. An addiction. When her tongue teased his lips, he almost lost control.

Kate felt bolder about trying some of the things she'd been thinking about for the past week. When she tasted his lips with her tongue, she noticed his breathing quickened. She wondered what it would be like to—Her thoughts made her cheeks burn, but not for long. Making love to Drew Kingman would be heavenly. She had no doubts about that now. Her guilt had been soothed away. Would he be as gentle as he'd been the other night? Would the fire she sensed in him, as his lips moved over hers, become a frenzy, or would he tantalize her mercilessly until she begged for—begged for what? Kate had no idea what she might beg for, but she'd heard the saloon girls talk enough to know they'd begged for something.

Drew ended the kiss. He suspected she would have kept kissing him for a lot longer if he'd persisted, but they had miles to cover and the going would be difficult, at best. It was getting to be more and more difficult to tell himself that kissing was all he was allowed to do with this woman. At least it would be cold tonight.

"We have to get moving." He brushed her hair back from her face and noticed her cheeks were flushed bright pink, just as Lucy's had been after they'd made love. Had Kate been thinking about it, too? He wished he could find out, but that wasn't part of the deal. A few kisses, maybe. Keeping each other warm at night, perhaps. But making love was another barrel of pickles entirely. Kate had hardly been ready to be kissed the first time. She surely wouldn't be able to cope with more. And with Carson out to kill him, he had no business getting tied up with Kate or any woman.

"Yes, it's time we got going." She didn't loosen her hold on him. Instead, she ran her fingers through the hair tumbling over his forehead. "I used to wonder if your hair was coarse or soft."

"Really?" Another minute. Then he'd push her away. Maybe two minutes.

"It's soft."

Laughter tumbled from him, echoing down the mountain, spooking a deer nibbling on a tender sapling. When the deer bounded into denser cover, Drew led Kate back to the horses and they resumed their journey.

Drew could hardly wait until dusk.

CHAPTER SEVEN

The going got slower with each passing hour. Drew knew it was too soon for such cold weather, and he knew the signs pointed to an early winter. Kate came right along behind him, every step of the way. By now, Lucy would have succumbed to exhaustion from the pace he'd set for them, but Kate never wavered in her determination to reach Silverton before her father died.

"Drew, may we stop, please?"

It was the first time since they'd left Laramie that she'd asked to stop before he'd decided it was time.

"What's wrong?"

"I . . . I can't breathe. Can't . . . get a deep . . . breath."

The altitude. Drew reckoned they'd climbed a good thousand feet in the past few hours, and the horses showed signs of tiring, too.

"Can you make it another fifteen minutes? There's a sheltered place up ahead where we can build a fire and rest a while."

She nodded, gasping for breath with her mouth open. Her face seemed pale, even in the cold.

Drew urged his horse on and felt resistance in the strong animals. If he continued to push ahead at this pace for much longer, the horses would lose their strength, and then they'd really be in a mess.

They reached the place Drew had spotted and he helped Kate from her horse. "Come over here and sit down. Put your head between your knees for a minute. The air is thin up here, that's a fact, but gasping won't help you take in more of it."

Kate nodded and tried to do as he'd said. Her head felt so light, so full of space, she feared she might keel over if she had to go much farther. But Drew was right. Slowing down, making herself take deeper breaths, helped immensely, and the dizziness soon left her. Drew had started a fire and was heating some water. Soon he'd have some coffee for them to drink. That would help, too.

"I'm sorry to be such a bother." She lacked enough breath to talk above a whisper.

"A bother? What sort of nonsense is that? You've been as hardy on this trail as any man. You've got nothing to apologize for." He hurried with the coffee. Within ten minutes, it was ready. "Here, drink this." He handed her a steaming cup of the strong, black brew.

She took it with a word of thanks and sipped it carefully. "We're not going to make it, are we?"

He ducked his head, then looked at her straight on. "No. But that cabin I told you about isn't much farther now. We'll be able to stay there until you've adjusted a bit more to the altitude. Then, maybe . . ."

"Who's kidding who?" she said with a smile. "With winter coming early this year, it was crazy for us to even try to get to Silverton before snowfall. Why did you agree to take me at all?"

Drew refused to look at her for a moment.

"Drew? Tell me the truth. Why did you say you'd do it?"

He sipped the coffee, adjusted his coat, and tipped his hat down over his eyes before he answered. "Because I wanted to stay with you, I guess."

Surprise showed on her face. "Even back in Laramie?"

"Before Laramie."

"Because I reminded you of Lucy?"

"I suppose that was part of it." He stood and tucked his cup back into the mule's pack. "I don't know. I didn't know then and I don't know now. What I do know is that I've gotten us into one hell of a—pardon—one bad predicament, and I'm going to be sorely pressed to get us out."

Kate couldn't help smiling. He'd wanted to be with her. Even if they froze to death in these mountains, holding each other, trying to stay warm—comforting each other—she would be satisfied. She'd never expected a man to admit he actually wanted to be with her, and hearing the words from this man was enough to put her in the best mood she'd been in since he'd kissed her earlier in the day.

"Do you think you can travel any farther, or should we make camp here?"

She felt better. The coffee had helped more than she expected. "I can go on a while longer. What time is it, do you suppose?"

Drew studied the position of the sun behind the clouds that had gathered thicker and darker since they'd reached the high country. "About four, I reckon. We'll try to go another hour, if you're up to it. We should get to that cabin pretty soon."

"You said it was twenty-five miles?"

"About that. We've been making pretty poor time since then, though. I don't like those clouds. It's only October, and already they're threatening snow. The high temperature every day won't climb much past thirty from now on."

Kate shivered. "I wish Silverton could be somewhere other than the mountains."

"That's where the silver is."

His words made a whole new batch of shivers dart down her spine. Did he know? He must have figured out that her father was a prospector, searching for gold or silver like every other fool in the country had been doing for the past twenty years. He didn't know yet that her father wasn't ill. At least she hadn't let that little parcel of information slip out. And he didn't know that her father, bless his black old shriveled heart, had struck it rich after twenty years. That part would be easier for him to hear, since it meant Drew would be paid for his trouble in getting her to Silverton. After that, he could go back to Texas and rebuild his ranch with the money he'd get from her pa. He'd go back to Texas . . .

"Why the long face?" Drew reached for her empty cup and packed it away with the rest of the gear.

"Oh, nothing, I guess. I was just thinking about my pa, that's all."

Drew frowned and touched her arm. "I'm sorry. We probably won't get there in time for you to see him. I'm really sorry."

His concern made her feel guilty. "I'm pretty sure he'll still be alive." She climbed back onto her horse. "He wouldn't dare die before we get there."

Drew squinted a little. There was something about the way she'd said it that made him suspicious. "What makes you think so?"

"Because he wired us he was dying with consumption. People don't usually die of consumption right away, do they?"

Drew studied her face and saw the color rise in her cheeks. She glanced at him quickly, then away at the clouds lazing on the mountainside ahead of them.

"No, they usually don't," Drew said slowly. "I thought you said your father was going to die real soon."

"He is! At least that's what he said. He probably will, if there aren't doctors and medicines close by. Does Silverton have a doctor?"

"I have no idea."

"Ben said he probably wouldn't live through the winter, prospecting and all. He's been searching for the 'mother lode' for nigh on twenty years. I doubt he'd give up his crazy dream of being rich just because of a little cough."

Did he believe the story? She couldn't tell without looking at him again, and she was afraid her expression would give the lie away, so she stared straight ahead—until Drew shifted his position straight in front of her so she had no choice but to look him in the eye.

"You told me your father was a man of wealth. Now, you say he's looking to get rich from silver. Which is it?"

Caught. "Both. That is, he was well-to-do when he left us. Maybe he lost everything and that's why he's prospecting now." Flimsy, and she knew it. She could tell he didn't believe a single word she'd said.

"All right, Kate. You demanded the truth from me. Now it's your turn. Your pa isn't dying in Silverton, is he?"

"Well, he could be."

Drew's face was getting redder by the minute. "But he isn't dying of consumption."

Kate couldn't lie anymore. What if he decided to leave her here to die? What would she do then?

"The truth!" He grabbed her by the shoulders and pulled her off her horse. "For once in your scrawny life, tell me the whole, damn truth! Is your father in Silverton?"

"Yes."

"Is he dying?" Rage made the veins on his temples stand out, pulsing.

"I don't know." Kate pulled away and turned her back to him, avoiding the eyes that bored into her like shards of ice. "They may have killed him by now. I don't know!"

"Killed him?" Some of the anger left his voice and his face cooled to a paler shade of red.

"Yes, killed him! I'm trying to get there before they kill him!"

"Who?"

"I don't know."

Kate got back on her horse, kicked him hard, and skirted around Drew. She didn't want to tell them they'd come on this ill-fated trip because of greed. Their lives might be in danger, all because she wanted her share of the money that could make her life bearable after all the years of poverty. In spite of everything they'd shared, she didn't know Drew well enough to predict what he'd say or do if he discovered her true reasons for wanting to get to Silverton.

Drew ran to catch up with her and grabbed the reins. "Whoa, there," he called to the horse, then pulled her down. The grip on her shoulders wouldn't be broken this time. "You're going to tell me everything. You hear me? Everything!"

Without warning, the side of the mountain came to life and tumbled toward them with the force of a Texas twister. Drew let go of Kate so abruptly, she almost fell.

"Rockslide!"

Kate screamed and searched frantically for a safe place to run to before the awful torrent of rock and dirt and debris could push her down the mountain. Drew yelled something, but she couldn't understand over the din. She spied a hollow in the cliff and dived toward it, pulling herself into as tight a ball as she could. Tears streamed down her cheeks, and fear for herself and Drew drove her into panic.

Then he was there with her. She pressed her face against his shirt and tried to hide from the choking dust. His body shielded her from branches and rocks barreling down on top of them from the surrounding cliffs. His body took the pounding for both of them.

Within a minute, the slide stopped and Drew sat up, dazed, and looked around to see what damage had been done.

"You all right?" He pulled her to her feet and peered into her eyes.

Gasping for breath, she nodded, and he left her to search for the horses and the mule. Without supplies and horses to ride, their situation could become even more perilous in a hurry.

Kate tried to see up the trail, where the slide had originated. Not a tree or shrub had been left standing. The face of the mountain had been wiped clean and nothing but rubble remained. The realization they could have been buried in all that debris made Kate shiver.

Drew came back, leading the horses. "The mule is dead, but most of the supplies are still usable. We'll have to pack what we can behind our saddles." He went to work dividing the load and secured everything on the horses. Whatever they could do without, he left behind to reduce and lighten the load.

Kate thought about the hard-working mule and tears came to her eyes. At least their supplies hadn't been lost. "I guess we'd better get on the way. Is that cabin nearby, do you think?"

"It should be. I hoped to reach it yesterday."

"Well, then, let's get moving. We don't have much time before dark." Kate got into the saddle with difficulty. Any energy she'd gained from their rest stop had been swept away with the face of the mountain. She hoped Drew wouldn't realize she hadn't answered his last question, about who was trying to kill her father, until they were on their way. Maybe he'd forget until they reached the cabin. By then, she might be able to come up with a believable story. She'd come too far to have him back out on her now.

Drew stepped up into the saddle with his mouth drawn into a tight line and an acrid taste in his mouth. That rockslide had proven mighty costly. And convenient, too, once he thought about it. It kept her from having to answer his questions, dammit. She was still lying to him, and it made him madder than tarnation! If her pa wasn't dying, then why the hell should he risk his life to get her to Silverton? And who in thunder was trying to kill her pa? When they got to the cabin, he'd have the truth, even if he had to shake it out of her.

They trudged on in silence until Drew decided she'd had enough for one day. He heard her wheezing and saw her bottom lip sagging. She was having a hard time breathing. Her breasts rose with each breath she took. Her breasts. Now why did he have to think about her breasts at a time like this? Here they were, about to pitch camp, and he had to go and think about her breasts! That's all he needed!

"Drew, look." She pointed. "Up ahead. Is that smoke?"

Drew stood in the stirrups. "It sure as shootin' is. There must be someone using that cabin. We'll share their fire tonight."

Kate nodded and smiled. The thought of sleeping out of the weather, maybe on a real bed, soothed her frazzled wits. She kicked up the horse, eager to be there at last.

They reached the cabin a quarter of an hour later. If only these folks wouldn't mind sharing the cabin with two cold, dirty, weary travelers, she and Drew would spend at least one night warm and sheltered.

Drew knocked on the door and they heard a scurry of voices and activity inside.

"Who's there?" came a rough voice.

"Andrew Kingman." Drew glanced at Kate. "My wife and I are headed toward Silverton. Can you spare us a corner for the night?"

Kate would have to play the part of Drew's wife again, for longer than before. The thought of it excited her in an odd, thrilling way. It would be as close to the real thing she'd ever know, that was for sure.

The cabin door squeaked open and Drew removed his hat. "I remembered this cabin as abandoned. Are you folks living here now?"

The man stepped back to let them come inside. "Nope. Just passing through. We'll be leaving directly."

Kate smiled at the man and his wife, who stood behind him as though she were afraid to let strangers share the cabin. Neither of them smiled back. Two small, ragged children huddled behind their mother's skirts.

"I'm Andrew Kingman." Drew held his hand out to the man. "This is my wife, Kate."

The man took Drew's hand and shook it heartily. "I'm William Bridger." He smiled from ear to grubby ear. "This here's my wife, Maude."

"Pleased to make your acquaintance," Maude said timidly.

"Same here." Kate dropped her gaze to the waifs still hiding in folds of worn calico. "You have lovely children."

The woman seemed to come alive. "Thank you, Mrs. Kingman."

The name hung in the air like clouds on the mountainside. Kate felt an empty place in her stomach she decided must be hunger.

"I'm Kate."

William ushered them over to the fire. "We've been here most of a week now. Jenny, Jacob, mind your manners. Get these people a chair. They must be tired."

Kate thanked little Jenny Bridger, who couldn't have been more than six, and dropped into the rough wooden chair the little girl dragged over from the table. Drew waved Jacob away, saying, "Thanks, but I'll stand."

"We have some stew if you're hungry." Maude hurried to tend the pot hanging over the fire. She grabbed the spoon sticking out of the pot and gave the contents a vigorous stir.

Kate's stomach rumbled at the same time Drew's did and they apologized in almost the same breath. That made everyone laugh.

"We've done et, so you're welcome to finish 'er up." William waved them to the table. The only other piece of furniture in the room was a bed in the corner that had a straw mattress a tad too small for the frame. The mattress, dirty and worn, had places where the stitching had come loose, letting dirty straw protrude from the gaps.

Drew sat down at the table across from Kate. "We were just about to set up camp when Kate saw the smoke from your chimney."

William picked up a huge log and pitched it into the fireplace. "This cabin ain't much to look at, but it's better than being out in the weather. Where were you folks when that slide turned loose a little while ago?"

"We were right under it."

Kate got up and took two full plates from Maude. The stew smelled delicious, even if the pot could've stood more scrubbing before it was prepared. Big chunks of meat swam in a thick brown gravy, with no vegetables she could see.

Kate set the plates on the table, then sat back down.

"We hate to take your only chairs." Drew started to get up.

"Oh, pshaw. Set a spell and take a load off."

Drew smiled and nodded. He turned to the plate of stew. Kate was already eating. From the expression on her face and the way she spooned bite after bite into her mouth, he decided the stew must taste as good as it smelled. After a bite, he agreed. Mighty tasty.

"So you folks are headed for Silverton?" The children huddled around Maude's feet again.

"Yes," Kate told her between bites. "I'm afraid we might not make it before the first snows, though."

"First snows won't fill the passes." William reached for a pipe and a pouch of tobacco. "We saw flurries this morning, early." He used a glowing stick from the fireplace to light the bowl and puffed clouds of blue smoke into the air. "It won't start to drift for a few days, anyway. You could make it just fine if you leave with us first thing in the morning. It's not that far."

Kate wished she could wave away the smoke that settled over the table and into their plates, but it would be bad manners to do so. Having spent so many hours in the saloon, cleaning spittoons, she'd had her fill of tobacco and smoke since she was a child. That was one thing she admired about Drew. He didn't seem to hanker for a smoke after every meal, the way most men did.

Drew coughed when the smoke surrounded him and fanned it away from his face.

"Sorry. Does the smoke get in your craw?" William's forehead creased right between his eyes.

"Sometimes, but it's not a problem." Drew looked back down at his plate, to the gravy he'd left.

Maude handed each of them a hard biscuit.

"Thanks, ma'am." He sopped up the last of the gravy. "That was mighty fine stew, ma'am. Real fine. What do you find up here for such a tasty stew?"

"Squirrel, mostly." She appeared pleased with his praise.

Kate added her compliments and offered to help wash the dishes.

"Oh, we don't wash 'em." Mrs. Bridger took the empty plates off the table. "I just wipe 'em and stack 'em."

Drew gave Kate a look that must have been exactly like the one on her face. How many times had the plates been used without being washed, or at least scrubbed with sand? Kate was glad she didn't know.

"Well, sun's going down. Best we get ready for bed." William yawned until Kate feared his cheeks would split. "You're welcome to put your horses in the shed out back with ours, where they'll be out of the wind. Give them some corn, too. There's a sack against the wall."

"Much obliged." Drew headed outside, and as he left, Kate

smiled shyly at Maude, who smiled back, revealing three teeth missing in front.

When Drew came back in, carrying the rest of their gear, he shivered over to the fireplace to warm his hands. "We'll just throw our blankets on the floor wherever there's room."

"The floor's all there is here, I'm afraid," Maude said apologetically. "Y'all could have the bed, I s'pose."

"The floor will be fine. We've been sleeping on the ground for days now. The floor will feel almost like a real bed."

But it didn't. The minute Kate lay down and felt the rough boards against her back, she knew she'd prefer a grassy spot or some pine boughs to the unyielding stiffness beneath her.

Drew settled down beside her. He draped his blanket over hers as they'd done before and eased his arm into place around her middle. Her back was to him, as usual.

"Tarnation, but this floor is hard," he whispered. They were at the far end of the room from the Bridgers, but still only about ten feet from the nearest sleeper.

"Just what I was thinking."

"What?" Drew propped up on one elbow.

Kate dropped back onto her shoulders so she could be heard. She found herself almost nose to nose with him. "I said, that's just . . . what I . . . was thinking." She made no move to turn back. Instead, she studied Drew's features without embarrassment and found there were parts of his face she'd never noticed before. The mole on his chin. A tiny scar just above his left eyebrow. She traced one finger across his forehead, looking for anything else she might have missed.

Slender fingers of flame licked the thick logs in the fireplace, and the crackle of the fire and the occasional pop, sending sparks up the chimney, were the only sounds in the room except for William's uneven snoring.

Drew pulled his hand up onto Kate's stomach. "Kate?"

"Hmmm?"

"Who's trying to kill your pa?" He moved his hand up to her face and trailed one finger down her cheek and under her chin.

"Let's talk about it later." She tried to ignore the tingling his fingers set up in her arms and legs and turned over again.

He pulled her back. "No, let's talk about it now. Who's trying to kill your pa?"

He wasn't going to let it go. Well, here in the cabin, where he couldn't yell and scream at her, might be the best place to get everything out in the open and straight between them.

"What if you start to yell again?" She touched the grizzled line of his jaw. It was a strong jaw, and, covered with several days' growth of beard; the way it was, it made her think of Ben, in a way. But Ben's jaw hadn't been nearly so square. And his beard, when it grew out, was dark instead of straw-colored like Drew's.

He nudged her. "I won't yell. Answer my question, woman."

"Claim jumpers." She waited for his reaction.

He stared at her.

"My pa struck it rich and claim jumpers are trying to push him off the claim. He sent for us to help him keep what's rightfully his—and ours." She waited.

Drew didn't move a muscle for at least a minute.

So, he thought, letting his fingers toy with one of the buttons on the front of her dress, the whole thing was built on lies. Her pa wasn't sick. He was just some old prospector who was afraid someone was going to push him off his claim. To get some help holding them off, he'd called for his kids—who weren't kids any longer—to come halfway across the country to help. There was no guarantee he'd actually found silver. In fact, Drew would bet his last two dollars the old man had lied. Kate was probably making this trip for nothing. And, Drew was making it for nothing, too, since there wouldn't be any money to pay him for his trouble once they got to Silverton. Only excuses and more lies, and probably a bucket of tears from Kate when she learned the truth. Damn. It wasn't right. Not right at all.

"Drew?" Kate ran her fingers up into his hair, right above his left ear. "Are you mad because I lied again?"

"Yep." He fingered the curls framing her face and marveled at how delicate her features seemed in the firelight.

She seemed apprehensive. "Are you carrying me high, or are you really mad?"

"I'm really mad." He kissed the tip of her nose.

"Stop that! I expected you to be boiling mad at me. Why aren't you?"

"Would it do any good?" He stroked the hair back from her face and kissed her earlobe, then sucked it into his mouth.

Kate ignored the question. With him nuzzling her ear, she couldn't concentrate on anything else. She ran her thumb around his ear and down his jaw to his lips. He kissed her thumb.

"I'm sorry I lied."

He kissed the rest of her fingers, one by one.

"You realize, I hope, that your pa may be the biggest liar of all."

"Pa? What are you talking about?"

"Would you have made the trip to Silverton if he hadn't struck it rich and needed help to protect his claim?"

"No, but—"

"Well, then . . ."

Kate's jaw fell open. She realized he could be right. She might be chasing an old fool's dream, right along with the old fool who'd abandoned them more than a decade ago.

"That old bastard . . ."

Drew placed one finger on her lips. He doubted she'd ever said such a word in her life, but it certainly fit the circumstances. "Let's not be calling your old man names until we know for sure. Have you told me everything?" He went back to her ear, circling it with his tongue, then breathed on the wet skin until she shivered.

"Everything I know. If there's more, we'll learn it together." When he leaned back, she added, "I'm sorry. I may have wrecked both our lives."

"You can be sorry if you want to. As for me, I'm rather enjoying this little jaunt through the mountains. Parts of it, that is." He was tired of whispering and nibbling earlobes and ready for something else. From the look in her eyes and the way her fingers sifted through his hair, sending tingles to places on his body a respectable lady would blush to think about, he thought Kate might be tired of talking, too.

Taking his time to build anticipation between them, he brushed his cheek against hers, then found her mouth. Her soft lips reminded him to be gentle. Thinking about her breasts earlier, right before they'd gotten to the cabin, had made him jumpy and irritable. It was time he did something about that. Past time.

The buttons gave way, one by one, until Drew knew there was plenty of room for his hand to slide in underneath. Plenty of room for his fingers to move around and tease and tickle a little. And, above all, he'd find out, once and for all, if her skin was as soft as he'd imagined. Would her nipples darken and gleam rosy red when touched—or kissed? Would she stop him? She hadn't so far, and he didn't think she would.

Kate enjoyed his sweet kisses and reminded herself they were merely comforting each other. That made it all perfectly all right. She really needed comforting tonight.

His right hand, which he normally rested on her waist, wasn't there. It was higher. And, instead of inching up to touch the soft swell of flesh pushing against the front of her clothes, his fingers were fumbling with the buttons on the front of the dress. Why, he was going to put his hand . . .

Kate panicked. She couldn't actually let him touch her bare skin, could she? It was what she'd thought about dozens of times. Hundreds of times. And now, when his hand was right there, about to slide inside her dress, about to . . . Oh, God, what should she do?

Drew waited for her to make up her mind. She lay stiff and still beside him and he knew there must be a powerful argument raging in her mind. But he just couldn't wait any longer. He'd give her one more chance to back out before going ahead, and if she backed out, that would be it. He'd never try to touch her again. Maybe she didn't want him to ask, though. Maybe, just like that first time, she wanted him to do it without asking, so she could preserve her dignity or her pride or whatever else it was she was preserving, by telling herself that it was he who had done the whole thing, with or without her consent. That it was all a part of the comforting. Yeah. That sounded good.

Kate wished he'd get on with it! He hovered there above her, almost as though he wanted her to give him permission. Well, she'd waited twenty-five years for this to happen, and she wasn't about to say no to it now!

"Drew?"

"Yes, Kate?"

"What are you waiting for?" She looked into his eyes with what she hoped was the right expression for such a request.

"I just wanted to be sure, that's all."

He smiled that gorgeous smile she'd come to watch for and slipped his hand inside her dress. She took a sharp breath when his fingers closed over her.

"Drew, I want you to understand why—"

"I understand, Kate. Believe me, I understand."

"I wouldn't want you to think—"

He kissed her to take her mind off what he was doing—and

to shut her up. His hand moved a little and she tensed, but then that same little noise came from her throat when he began to stroke and rub, loving the feel of her, getting to know the shape that had driven him crazy for days. He knew he had to look at her. Before she could say anything, he peeled the dress back and admired the soft skin his hand was touching.

Kate felt a wave of embarrassment when Drew's eyes moved down from her face. A man was actually seeing her without her clothes! Before she could get used to him looking at her that way, he lowered his mouth to her left nipple, which already stood up, hard and warm, and his tongue wet the dusky skin while his other hand caressed and kneaded.

"Oh, Drew, Drew." She pulled her knees up, compelled to roll herself into a tight little ball. Such feelings! She'd never have been able to imagine the ecstasy of such a caress.

"Shhh." His breath on the wet nipple made it stand out even more. "There are children across the room."

All four Bridgers were snoring now, but Kate wasn't listening. She ran her fingers through his hair while he tasted her nipple again and again.

"Drew?" She'd go to hell for this for sure.

He didn't raise his head this time. "What?"

"I have another one." She knew she should be ashamed of her brazenness, but she ached to have him give the other breast the same splendid attention he'd lavished on the first one.

His smile lit up the room, and he kissed her deeply, thoroughly, while he pulled her dress back on the other side. "Kate, you're quite a woman." He commenced to repeat on the right what he'd done on the left, and marveled at the fact that she was fuller, firmer, softer than he'd ever imagined from looking at her fully clothed. That dress must be really tight to minimize her virtues the way it did. He vowed then and there to buy her a new dress once they got to Silverton.

Kate found it impossible not to cry out. The shocks and tingles running through her body were so wonderful, the sounds coming from her throat came involuntarily, and when Drew shushed her again, she buried her face in his shoulder, hoping he wouldn't quit because she was being so noisy.

His heart pounded in his ears. He wanted to touch her—all over. Kiss her—all over. Bury himself inside her. But he knew she wasn't ready, and that here in a cabin with four other people wasn't the place to introduce Kate to all the joys of lovemaking. With difficulty, Drew stopped sucking her nipples and rolled away, breathing hard, as if he'd run a mile in less than a minute.

Kate opened her eyes. "Drew, what's wrong?"

He tried to think of branding calves, of toiling in a silver mine, of rattlesnakes and scorpions—anything but the woman lying submissive beside him, making her damned little noises, driving him crazy—crazy!

"Drew?" She was worried now. Worried she'd displeased him somehow. But, the look on his face when he turned back eased her mind. "Why did you stop?" she asked innocently. "It felt wonderful."

"Because if I don't stop now, I won't be able to stop." He stared into the fire again and thought about cutting calves.

"I don't understand. Why wouldn't you be able to stop whenever you choose to?"

He looked at her hard. "Are you really that innocent?" He wanted to reach for her breast again, but he shoved his hand in his pocket instead and tried not to look at her creamy flesh, golden in the firelight, tantalizing him with its virgin blush. "Have you never been told what men and women do after they're married?"

"Well, I've heard bits and pieces from the girls in the saloon. They talk about—I can't tell you what they talk about. It's too . . . well . . . too personal."

Drew shook his head. She'd let him kiss her breasts but she couldn't talk about anything personal.

"Kate, I'm going to ask you a question. You don't have to answer it if you don't want to. Do you know what sex is?"

Kate's cheeks flamed crimson when she heard the word. "Of course I know what it is."

"Do you know how it's done?"

Kate glared at him. "Of course I know. Do you think I'm nothing more than a child?" She buttoned the bottom button on her dress, then unbuttoned it again.

Drew nodded. "All right. I just didn't know for sure. What I said before, about not being able to stop—" He glanced down at her breasts and saw that her nipples were still erect. Damn! He didn't have this much will power, did he? Did any man?

Kate had told him she wasn't a child, but that's exactly what she felt like. Why had she been so stupid? She'd thought of making love to him, without stopping to consider that he might think about the same thing! And he obviously was thinking of that very thing—right now. She turned away and tried not to cry. She never expected any man would want to make love to her. It was too wonderful for words. If only she could stop crying, she'd tell him it wasn't necessary for him to stop.

When he felt the sobs shake her slender frame, he touched her cheek with one finger. "Kate, look at me."

"No." She tried not to blubber but it was no use.

"Please?"

She turned toward him and dried her tears on his shirt. "Hold me."

Drew gathered her tight against him and kissed her eyelids and her cheeks and the tip of her nose, then her mouth, because she was making more noise than a calf cut off from its mother at roundup time, and he had to shut her up somehow. He also buttoned her dress all the way to the top.

"Let's get some sleep." He pushed her over on her side, and took several long, slow deep breaths, trying to calm down. He'd pushed her too far. Fool! Couldn't he see she wasn't ready?

Kate wished she could hold him and run her fingers through his hair again, and tell him she wanted him to make love to her, but he'd turned away, completely away, and she feared he wouldn't come back. She'd made a moron of herself, that's what she'd done, and she'd pay for it someday.

"Good night, Drew," she whispered.

He didn't answer.

Chapter Eight

Mrs. Bridger fixed a huge breakfast of corncakes and molasses and white bacon fried in a skillet over the fire. They all shared the meal. After Maude had wiped the plates clean and stored them in a pack, William gathered his trappings and ushered his family out the door.

"Glad to have made your acquaintance, Kate," Maude said timidly.

"Same here, Maude." Kate saw loneliness in the woman's eyes and wished they could've gotten to be friends. Kate had a feeling it had been a long time since Mrs. Bridger had had another woman to talk to.

Drew helped with their horses and pack mule. "There's a good hotel in Laramie. The Prancing Horse. Owned by the McGruders. Tell them you saw us. They're good people."

Kate's chest swelled with tightness at the memory of Meg's kindness to her. "Tell Meg thanks for all she did for us."

"We'll tell her." Mr. Bridger helped his wife onto her horse, then put the children on another horse. He turned to Drew and offered his hand in parting. "I hope you make Silverton before blizzard."

"Thanks. I hope so, too."

It was noticeably colder this morning, and the wind had shifted to the north. Kate hugged herself to block the wind as much as she could.

With a wave and a command to the horses, the Bridgers

headed down the trail. Before long, in the thick tangle of foliage, they disappeared.

Drew refused to look straight at Kate until they were completely out of sight, and then he did so only to tell her he was going out to look around and see what sort of chance he thought they had of making it to Silverton before snow. Kate could tell he was still angry about last night, but she had no idea whatsoever what she should do about it, so she applied herself to the task of tidying up the cabin in case they had to stay another night.

Another night. What would it be like with the two of them in the cabin alone? Somehow, it seemed different from being alone together outside, in the open, where any person or animal might happen on their camp. Here they had privacy, and privacy meant . . . well, she didn't want to think about what it meant.

An old broom leaned against the corner next to the fireplace, and Kate worked off a good bit of her frustration on the rough split-log floor for the next hour. The place needed a good cleaning, and if there was one thing Kate had learned to do while growing up, it was clean.

A swirl of dust and debris clouded out the door, then she looked around to see what needed attention next. There were some shelves on the wall next to the fireplace, cluttered with a collection of pots and pans Kate had assumed were the Bridgers'. Thank goodness they belonged with the cabin. Outside, the wind howled through the trees. Kate shivered and felt thankful they weren't out in it.

All in all, it was quite a cozy little cabin, stocked with everything a body needed, except fresh meat. They wouldn't have to worry about that, since they'd be leaving soon for Silverton. The supplies they'd brought, plus the scant remains in the cabin, would keep them fine.

Drew came in and headed straight for the fireplace. "It's getting colder out there. We'll have snow before morning." His teeth chattered. He held his hands out to the flames to warm them and never once looked straight at her.

"Snow? Already?" Kate couldn't help the sound of frustration in her voice. They'd come so far. They couldn't go back now! All their talk about having to spend the winter in the cabin had been just that to Kate—talk. She never once believed they weren't going to make it all the way.

"Kate, we shouldn't have tried this fool stunt in the first place. I knew it and you probably knew it, too. We can probably make it, but it's going to be rough. If you want to go back to Laramie, we'd best be getting to it."

Kate's eyes stung with tears. How dare the weather treat her so badly? Every person she'd ever known in the world had treated her badly. The weather had no business doing it, too! She turned away from Drew and dropped into one of the rough, straight-backed chairs at the table and covered her face with her hands.

Drew glanced over and his throat tightened at the sight of her sitting there, crying over what amounted to his blunder. Dammit, he never should've told her he'd take her to Silverton in the first place. He knew it was too late in the year to set out on such a trip, but he'd given in to his gut feelings—or, if he'd admit it, to some feelings a little lower—and now they were going to have to go through some rough territory in order to get to Silverton before the first blizzards. He knew she wouldn't want to go back. She had too much spunk for that. So, what choice did he have?

"Kate, we're low on provisions," he said solemnly. "I'll have to rustle up some meat before we head out again. It'll take me a day—maybe two. That'll make the trip harder, but that's the way it is. I got us into this mess and I'll get us out. Snow is fixing to fall like cotton off a cottonwood tree. It's a little early, but not much. But early or not, there's nothing you or I can do about it." Drew whirled around and stared straight into her eyes, bracing himself for a tantrum. What he saw surprised and puzzled him. She was smiling.

Kate got up from the chair and took one step closer to him, then two steps back. She couldn't be near him right now. If she got too close to him, she didn't know what would happen.

"I understand," she said. "Of course we'll do whatever you think is best."

Drew's forehead wrinkled and his eyes narrowed. "You aren't mad?"

"What good would it do? I'll help get some food ready to travel. When the time comes to leave, we'll leave, and we'll make it. Unless you'd rather head back to Laramie. I'll understand if you don't want to take me on to Silverton. After all, I brought you on this trip under false pretenses."

Drew didn't know what to say next. Damned woman. Just when he thought he had her figured out, she went and pulled this on him. Why wasn't she raging mad? Stomping and yelling and accusing him of bringing her into the mountains when they had no business here? Why wasn't she demanding to be taken on to Silverton, or back to Laramie, or . . . or anywhere in the world except where they were? How on earth could he stay in this cabin with her for another night without . . . Drew turned back to the fire and tried to get a grip on himself. He'd expected her to be furious, and now here he was furious instead. Damn. His life had really taken a turn for the worse when he'd crested that ridge in Wyoming.

Kate eased past him toward the kettle hanging over the fire. The rest of the stew, left over from last night, hissed and bubbled over the fire. She reached for the poker and pulled the arm holding the kettle out of the fireplace so the stew wouldn't stick and burn. He still wouldn't look at her. "Drew? What's wrong? Can't you tell me?"

Drew took several deep breaths before answering. "Nothing is wrong, Kate. Nothing at all. I've got to lay in a supply of meat for us, and the woodpile needs some fortifying, too. We'll be here at least one more night and probably two. Is there anything you need before I go? I won't be back until dark."

Alone in the cabin until dark. Well, Kate had certainly spent her share of time alone after Ben had married. Being alone was one thing she could do right well. But Drew leaving her alone distressed her. "I'll be fine," she said, braving a smile. "Will you bring something to cook for supper, or should I fix something from what's left of our supplies?"

"If I'm not back by dusk, fix whatever you want for yourself. Don't worry about me."

Don't worry about him? Did he actually think she wouldn't? She tried to smile, but it came out crooked and warped into a frown before she could do a thing to stop it.

"Kate, are you sure you'll be all right here while I'm gone? There's a bar on the door. Don't let anyone in until I get back, all right?"

"All right. Don't worry about me. I'll be fine." She stirred the stew again. "Do you want some stew before you go?"

"I'll eat some jerky on the way. If I'm to round up some meat for us, I need to get to it now." He ambled over to the door and put his coat on, then pulled his hat down to a line just above his eyebrows.

"I'll have some coffee made when you get back."

He smiled and let himself look at her for a moment. "That'd be right nice." Damn, but she was a good-looking woman. "Right nice," he said again, feeling like a schoolboy talking to the schoolmarm. But this was no schoolmarm. He didn't know exactly what sort of life she'd led back in Sutterfield, but he could tell it hadn't been a good one. And he also knew—just how, he couldn't rightly say—they'd treated her wrong. This woman was a real lady. She just hadn't ever been given a chance to show it. He wanted to kiss her again. Hold her again. Make love to her for the rest of the day. "I'll be back." He closed the door behind him.

Kate stifled the urge to cry, then gave in to it. Crying over a man, for goodness sake! But he treated her . . . well . . . like a lady. Like one of the fine ladies back home or in Laramie or Denver or San Francisco. With a shuddering sigh, Kate swiped at the tears and snuffled over to the door. Kate had a feeling, if she and Drew could just get to Silverton before her old fool of a father lost his claim, her luck would change. Yesiree, Bob, it would change. She wanted Drew to share in that good fortune. After what he'd gone through to get her even this far, he deserved it.

The thick stew had scorched a bit, but Kate ate it anyway, then took the pot outside to look for a stream or some sand to clean up with. Hadn't Mr. Bridger mentioned something about a stream fairly close to the cabin? Maybe she could hear it if she stood real quiet for a minute.

The wind, shimmering through the aspen leaves, made a soft whushing sound that harmonized with all the other sounds coming from the forest. Birds sang as though the first snow was an event they relished. Squirrels screeched and scolded one another, and Kate, too, for interrupting their caching away nuts and berries and whatever morsels they could fit into their bulging cheeks.

Kate closed her eyes for a moment and took a long, deep breath. The cold, sharp air reminded her of the barber's razor after he'd slapped it across the strap to sharpen it. That wind could slice through whoever might fall victim to its cutting edge. She thought about Drew with his coat up around his ears. He needed a scarf. If only she had some wool and some needles, she'd knit one for him.

A smile widened until she laughed with sheer joy. Drew. The only man ever to find her pretty. The only man ever to touch her in such intimate ways. The only man ever to want to make love to her. The only man . . .

Her smile faded. Would he truly be the only man in her life who would want her the way he'd wanted her last night? And what did she want? A home? A husband? Children? Certainly. All women wanted such things, didn't they? But the last thing in the world she wanted was to marry a miner. Her mother had had such a husband and what did it get her? Pain and misery, that's what. The last few years of her life spent alone, trying to raise two small children. Well, Kate knew better. She'd never fall in love with a miner. And since she would have to live in a mining town, filled with nothing but miners, she might as well accept that she was destined to be a maiden lady forever. No husband. No children. A mining shack where she'd care for her father until his death, if he hadn't already died before she and Drew could get there. If Pa had died, she'd be completely alone, and stuck in a putrid mining town.

Fear clutched at her heart and she stamped her foot against it. "He's not dead! He's alive!" He just had to be alive.

The sound of water tripping over stones on its way down the rugged mountainside reached her on the wind. She turned all the way around to test for direction. Following the sound, she found the stream about fifty yards from the cabin. It wasn't much, but it would provide water for drinking, and an occasional spit bath.

She cleaned the pot in the icy water, knowing it would be harder to get water after the stream froze over. She filled the pot as full as she could carry and headed back toward the cabin.

Inside, she hung the pot on the arm of the fireplace, dipped some clear, cold water into one of the cooking pans, and saved the rest for drinking. Before Drew got back, she was determined to have a bath, even if it meant using only a few cups of water. With a smile and a tilt of her head, she hummed "Buffalo Gals," one of the saloon songs she'd heard a thousand times, and rummaged in Drew's backpack for a bar of soap.

CHAPTER NINE

Drew had no trouble finding game. And spoilage didn't pose any problem with the temperature dropping the way it was. The meat could be cached outside the cabin and kept frozen until they needed it. The stream he'd crossed coming from the cabin ran fast enough to keep them in water for a good long while— until it eventually froze. The horses could graze and make do on whatever forage grew near the cabin, and drink from the stream. When it got too cold, he and Kate might have to eat one of the horses, but he hoped it wouldn't come to that.

All in all, it wasn't a bad setup. And peaceful. Mighty peaceful. Except for that woman. When it came to thinking about her, his mind and his loins felt anything but peaceful. He still hadn't decided what he was going to do about her when a buck bounded into a clearing just ahead, twitching his ears beneath a rack of eight points.

Drew eased the rifle into place at his shoulder. Taking care not to breathe deeper than a rabbit being stalked by a fox, he took aim and squeezed the trigger.

The deer leapt into the air at the sound of the shot, but the bullet found its mark. The buck fell, quivered its last, and Drew felt the usual sadness that came with killing such a beautiful animal. This particular buck, though, meant food for himself and Kate for a good many days.

Drew dressed the carcass, looped a rope around the rack,

then started back toward the cabin, dragging the deer behind him.

Snow fluttered around him, first in tiny flakes, then in ever-larger ones. By morning they'd be snowed in. He was lucky to have spotted this buck so soon. Otherwise, they might've gotten pretty hungry before he could get out to hunt again.

The rope dug into his shoulder, so he shifted it to the other side. Smoke from the chimney swirled among the snowflakes and reminded him that Kate waited back at the cabin.

His discomfort began immediately and refused to abate, even when he thought about pulling the heads off chickens. There was no avoiding the truth. Drew wanted to make love to Kate. Here on this mountain. Right now. Today. It was bound to happen sooner or later. Why suffer this frustration any longer than absolutely necessary?

But then, he thought, moving the rope back to the other shoulder, Kate might have different ideas. She'd seemed willing enough last night until he'd mentioned not being able to stop. Then, she'd started to cry. Dagnabbit! Why did women have to be so golderned hypocritical? First, she wants to be kissed and touched, then she doesn't. She says she knows about sex, but can't talk about such sensitive matters, even when he's kissing her nipples.

Her nipples. Hard as little rocks under his tongue. Dusky and dark compared to her lily-white skin that had never known sunshine. And her lips. Swollen after being kissed, as though they weren't used to such activity. And they weren't, dammit! Just because she liked having her breasts rubbed and kissed a little didn't mean she'd want to have anything else rubbed . . . and touched . . . and kissed . . .

He put the rope down and worked his eyes with the heels of both hands. Torture, that's what it was. Thinking about her like this was sheer torture. What he wanted might not be what she wanted. He'd learned that the day he'd met her. The first day. Lying in the dust. About to be bitten by a five-foot rattler.

Drew shuddered at the memory and shouldered the rope again. The deer seemed to be getting heavier the farther he went.

If he made up his mind that today was the day, and approached her with the intention of teaching her everything there was to know about making love, what if she backed off and said, "Don't touch me!" What then? Should he forget it? Forget it and live with her in a cabin so small that neither of them could breathe without feeling the warmth of the other's breath?

Kate's breath. Soft on his cheek, on his neck, against his mouth.

Stop it, Kingman! he scolded himself. *You're just making things worse.*

Kate's fingers combing through his tangled hair. Brushing his beard. Outlining his lips. Her eyes. Smoky blue, like the pinfeathers of a jaybird. Clear as a bell when angry. Hazy and soft when he kissed her.

Today. It had to be today. If she said no, then tomorrow, or the day after. But it had to be soon. No, not soon. Now. When he got back to the cabin.

He hadn't had a bath in a week. Not exactly how he'd choose to present himself to her the first time. Right now, he wouldn't blame her if she pinched her nose and pushed him away. No, when he showed her how pleasurable it could be to love someone, by being so close they couldn't get any closer unless they melted together and became one body, he wanted to be reasonably clean and as sweet-smelling as he could ever expect to be.

He smiled. That's how it would be. When he and Kate joined in love, they'd feel like one person instead of two. They'd give pleasure to each other and when it was over . . . What then?

Drew frowned. Things would get complicated in a hurry. Once they'd made love, he'd want to make love to her every day. And she might want to make love to him every day, too. The thought brought a smile. He scratched his whiskered chin. He'd get rid of this beard first so he could feel her skin against his bare face. And, he'd take a bath, even if he had to do it in that icy stream. He'd be as gentle as if he were helping birth a calf worth a hundred dollars. And Kate wouldn't turn away. She'd turn toward him and maybe say, "What are you waiting for?" just like she did last night, and—

Drew quickened his pace as much as the heavy carcass would allow. The cabin was only about thirty yards away now. He'd made up his mind. He knew the decision was a good one.

The cold couldn't penetrate his clothes now. Beneath his shirt and coat and underclothes, he felt warm with desire for the woman who had fallen into his life from the back of a bay horse. A woman who had pushed out the loneliness of living alone and filled his innards with happiness again. A woman he wanted to be with for the rest of his life.

A woman who was screaming at the top of her lungs.

CHAPTER TEN

Having swept the rough wooden floor until she could raise no more dust, Kate decided to wash the table, chairs, shelves and hearth. Anything to keep her mind from dwelling on the situation at hand. Anything to keep her thoughts from straying to Drew and the intimacies they'd shared the night before.

Kate stopped cleaning and closed her eyes, remembering the feel of his lips on her skin, his tongue circling each nipple, his fingers teasing and stroking, making her want to cling to him, to pull him closer until they were more like one person than two.

Now that it was clear they'd be in this cabin for weeks, Kate flushed crimson, imagining what that could mean. Drew wouldn't want to stop next time, if she allowed a next time to occur. She knew she would. How could she refuse his sweet attentions when she craved them above all else? How could she deny herself the adoration of a man when there would never be another? Even if another man showed interest, she knew she could never feel the same about him as she'd come to feel about Drew. How could she wait another day, another hour, to feel his hands and mouth on her, to know what it was to be loved totally?

Why hadn't he come back? Surely he'd been able to find game by now. What if he didn't come back until tomorrow? He had to!

She'd fix the best supper she could manage with such meager rations. Then, a pallet in front of the fireplace. After that, whatever he wanted, she'd oblige. Willingly. Eagerly.

Kate smiled and touched her lips with her fingertips. They already felt swollen with desire for his kisses. She reached lower, to her belly, and wondered for the hundredth time what it would feel like if he touched her there.

"Land sakes! I'm never going to have this place clean if I don't stop daydreaming!" She attacked the hearth again with a vengeance and scrubbed at layers of soot and grime collected over years of neglect.

She had to have some water to do justice to the hard cleaning. She grabbed a bucket and her coat and bundled herself against the cold.

Outside, she lifted her face to the downy flakes peppering her eyelids, melting on her tongue. They'd be snowed in by morning. Unable to leave the cabin.

Would they have enough to eat? She'd better try to spot edible plants and berries on her way to fetch the water. She might even find some tubers if she kept a sharp eye out for them.

Stream water fussed over and around the rocks, worn clean by constant bathing. The chatter of a squirrel punctuated the babble, along with the cry of a blue jay. Kate put the bucket down and leaned close to the surface of the water to scoop up a handful to drink. The sweet, frigid water numbed her hands and the inside of her mouth as it quenched the thirst she'd built up during the cleaning.

With a smile, she reminded herself that Drew would quench the other thirst within her. Tonight.

Bending to scoop another handful, she heard a snuffling in the undergrowth on the far side of the stream. It reminded her of a dog, burrowing through a trash pile.

"Drew, is that you?" She burst out laughing when she realized she'd just compared Drew to a rummaging dog.

Her laughter dried up to stilled panic when she saw the source of the noise.

Dark, shaggy fur. Small ears, laid back next to a flattened skull. Black, piercing eyes roaming the area, alert to the presence of any living thing nearby. Fangs, dripping with the juices of its cavernous red mouth. Claws as long as the tines of a fork.

Kate froze, trying not to breathe, trying to blend into the stream bank, praying that the faint breeze swirling ever-larger snowflakes around her face wouldn't carry her scent to the grizzly, giving her away.

The bear seemed oblivious to Kate, yet those cold eyes rested on her from time to time as if to say, "I know you're there. I'll get to you in a minute."

Kate felt her boot slipping on the mossy turf of the stream bank and leaned back, hoping to keep her balance. A mistake.

A chunk of sod broke off and plunged her right boot into the icy water. Her arms flailed as she tried to find balance. She let out a cry when the frigid water poured over the top of her boot, soaking her foot to the skin.

The bear roared and lunged at her.

Kate screamed, scrambling away from the stream.

Claws and teeth bared, the grizzly lumbered toward her, unrushed, certain of its ability to bring down such puny prey.

Kate grabbed the bucket and hurled it at the monstrous bear, only yards away.

The bucket bounced off the bear's snout and it howled with pain and fury, teeth dripping saliva, gushing at the sight of prey.

The trees around Kate stretched into the gray sky overhead, providing no lower limbs she could climb. She'd become bear food in a hurry if she tried to reach the lower limbs. Her only hope lay in getting back to the cabin, but the bear gained with every lumbering leap. She'd never make it in time.

Kate screamed again and again, stumbling and falling, knowing that any second the bear's teeth and claws would sink into her flesh.

A gunshot tore through her panicked mind. The roar of the beast, almost on top of her now, drowned all other sounds. Another shot. Drew shouted her name. Then screams. Not hers. His.

Kate watched in terror when the bear lunged at Drew, driving him to the ground. Blood covered them both and spread over the newly fallen snow. Then the bear slumped over Drew's body, quivered, then lay still.

CHAPTER ELEVEN

Kate scrambled to her feet, crying, clutching at her skirts, screaming at Drew, who lay as still as the dead bear.

"Drew, you can't be dead, you can't!" Sobs choked her. Tears blinded her. Fear stabbed at her heart.

No response came from Drew or from the heap of fur covering him. Kate staggered over to where she could see Drew's face. He'd been slashed across the forehead. Blood ran into his eyes and down his cheeks, glistening red and sticky. The wind had picked up and felt like needles on her bare skin.

Kate heaved against the bear's body until it shifted off Drew and tumbled down the slope, crushing a sapling as it fell.

Drew lay as still as death. Kate saw blood everywhere on his torn body, but the wound gushing dangerously was on his right thigh, about eight inches above the knee. The bear's claws had torn clear to the bone. If she couldn't stop the bleeding, all chances of saving his life would be lost.

Kate tore a strip of cloth from her skirt and tied it tightly around Drew's thigh, just above the wound. Drew groaned with pain when she pulled it down into a hard knot.

"You're alive!" She collapsed onto his chest, sobbing with relief.

"You're suffocating me, woman!" He tried to get up, but it proved impossible. He grabbed his head and fell back. "Damn, but that hurts. Is the bear dead?"

"Yes. Yes, you killed it. I thought it had killed you, too."

"You ought to know by now I'm tougher than any bear." He tried to sit up again but she held her hands to his chest to prevent him.

"Don't try to move. Please! I . . . I'll get you back to the cabin somehow. Just don't move. If your leg bleeds any more, you'll . . . you'll . . ." The words turned to sobs and she leaned over him, easing her arms beneath his shoulders, trying to hold him closer, begging him not to die.

Drew raised one grimy, bloody hand to her hair and stroked it gently off her face. "Kate, I'm not going to die. You mustn't carry on so about me. You'd think we were . . ."

Kate finished the sentence for him with a stern look that warned him he'd better not try to move again. "Married? You think I'm acting like your wife instead of some poor defenseless woman you reluctantly volunteered to escort halfway across the country? Is that it?"

Drew smiled. "Yep. But it's kinda nice to have a woman fuss over me again."

The quiet, unspoken reference to his dead wife washed over Kate like the icy water of the stream. Kate wasn't Drew's wife, and there was no reason to ever believe she might be. For the time being, though, she was all he had, and she'd have to do.

"Fuss over you? Not on your life, Mr. Kingman." She tried to feign indignation. "I'll tend your wounds and nurse you back to health, but I assure you, it isn't because I'm feeling wifely toward you. On the contrary. If you're to escort me to Silverton come springtime, you must be able to travel and defend me against attackers." Drew was smiling. "What, may I ask, is so amusing?"

"You. As soon as you're finished with that highfalutin' speech, you might think about getting me back to the cabin. That artery won't hold long with just that flimsy piece of skirt around it. And the dirt mixed in all these wounds will cause festering if it isn't cleaned out pretty soon. So, can you stop lecturing me long enough to get us home?"

Home. Kate felt a flush of embarrassment and pleasure at hearing that word. "Of course. Can you stand?"

"If you'll help me . . ."

Drew looped his arm around her neck and shoulders. "My hands aren't torn up too much, but my leg seems to be in bad shape."

"It's a deep wound." Kate grunted with lifting his weight and staggered when he pulled his left leg beneath him, trying to find purchase on the muddy, steeply sloped ground.

"Can you hold me?"

"Lean on me. I'm stronger than I look."

"That you are," he said softly.

The change in his tone startled her and she gasped at the shine in his eyes. Love? Certainly not. Admiration, maybe. Appreciation, surely. But love? Impossible.

"Let's take it a few steps at a time." She felt his hand tighten on her shoulder, once, twice, before he took his first step and cried out with the pain shooting through his leg. She stopped to let him catch his breath.

"It's all right now. Let's try it again." He leaned harder on Kate, hopping on his left leg, holding his right off the ground the best he could.

Kate could see blood seeping from beneath the tourniquet and knew they had to stop the flow soon or Drew could bleed to death.

"God, help me," she pleaded, and held Drew tighter.

Half an hour later, they reached the door of the cabin. Drew slumped inside the door with Kate behind him, breathing laboriously. The warmth of the cabin felt like a furnace after being outside in the frigid wind.

When her breathing eased, Kate tore strips from her petticoat, then dumped them into the stew pot. She added water, then stuck the pot over the flames in the fireplace to boil. She'd have to bring more water, and soon. Those rags had to be clean before she put them on Drew's wounds.

"Kate!"

She ran to where Drew had collapsed on the floor and eased her rolled up coat beneath his head. "What is it?"

"Leg. Hurts. Got to move. Get it straight."

She tried to help him get his leg into a more comfortable position. Blood had soaked his pants and pooled on the floor beneath him. "I'm boiling some rags for a bandage." Her tears rolled down her cheeks and soaked into his bloody shirt. His breathing seemed to stop for a moment before he took a rasping breath and let it out with a shudder. "You can't die. Please don't die."

Drew touched her bowed head. "I'm not gonna die, but I might pass out if you don't loosen that cinch on my leg."

"Of course." Kate swiped at her tears, then reached for the blood-soaked strip of cloth that had made a blue line around Drew's thigh. When she loosened it, the wound began to flow again, but not as vigorously as before.

He let out a long sigh. "That's better."

Kate heard the water boiling in the pot. "I'll get the bandages, and something to pack the wound, put pressure on it, so it'll clot." She tightened the cloth again. He groaned.

Kate fished the rags out of the pot with a stirring stick and laid them on the table. The dry wood soaked up a lot of the water immediately, and Kate wondered if her efforts to get them clean had been wasted once she'd laid them on the table, but there was no time to redo any of it now. That wound had to be packed and tied so the tourniquet could be removed completely.

When Kate got back to Drew, he seemed to be asleep, but

woke up instantly when she poured warm water into the wound to flush it, then packed it firmly with a folded cloth. Two strips around the pad held it in place. Then she wrapped the entire leg with strips to cover the numerous slashes and cuts he'd sustained.

"You look like you've done this before." The wrinkles in his forehead eased a bit.

"Lots of times. When you grow up in a saloon—" She stopped, angry that she'd revealed a part of her past she'd intended never to mention.

Drew sensed her discomfort, but still wondered how she'd come to be raised in a saloon. Was she the owner's daughter, or the daughter of one of the saloon girls? That was the most likely explanation. It would also explain why Kate was so belligerent about accepting help from anyone, and was so tight-lipped about her personal life. Tainted from birth, she would've had to fight her way through life. It explained a lot.

"There. It's done. Now we have to get you onto a pallet near the fire so you won't get chilled. Pretty soon, the fever is going to start and I have to get out and find some healing herbs to brew a tea to stem that fever."

"You know about healing, too?"

Kate looked him square in the eyes. "I know a lot of things, Drew." She got up from the floor. "I'll make that pallet for you, then I'll get the herbs." She'd begun to repeat herself but couldn't help it. She was consumed with worry about what Drew must think of her, now that she'd let it slip about the saloon. Drew might think she'd been one of the saloon girls. If he did, he'd be confused for sure, since she'd been so naïve that first night he'd kissed her. She shook her head a little and reminded herself that it didn't matter what Drew thought. Right now, her only concern was keeping Drew alive during the days to come, when he was going to be sicker than he'd ever been in his life. The herbs—if she could find them—would help only a little. It would be a long night. She hoped he'd be alive come morning.

All through the first night, then the second, Kate tended Drew's injuries. His fever, when morning seeped in around the door-frame after the third night, had come down a little but still gave cause for worry. Once again, Kate dipped one of the rags in the cool water she'd laboriously hauled from the stream—terrified another bear would see her and they'd both die—then wrung it out and placed it on Drew's forehead.

"Kate?" Drew's voice, almost a whisper, reflected the misery he'd endured.

"I'm here." The hallucinations he'd suffered during the worst part of the fever had taught her that just because he called her name, it wasn't proof he even knew she was in the room with him.

"Water." He tried to lick his parched lips, but his tongue stuck to the ragged skin.

Kate reached for a tin cup, dipped some of the drinking water, and lifted Drew's head just enough to drizzle a few drops between his lips. During the night she'd done the same, trying to moisten his mouth without giving him enough to make him choke. The fever had consumed every drop she'd managed to give him.

"Thanks," he muttered. "How long did I sleep?"

"Sleep?" She wouldn't call what he'd been through "sleep." "Going on three days now, since you killed the bear."

"Three days?"

"You passed out. Then the fever—"

"I get the picture. Am I gonna live?"

"You promised me you would. How could I get to Silverton without you?" Her words held no sting. She sifted his damp hair lovingly with her fingers.

"Sorry, ma'am. No way to get to Silverton today. Maybe tomorrow."

"Be kind of hard with three feet of snow on the ground and more falling all the time."

Drew's mouth tightened into a line. "I was afraid of that. I'm truly sorry, Kate. I hope your father—"

"My father will be fine. He's taken care of himself without me for a lot of years. He can do it a few more weeks."

Drew began to remember, in bits and pieces, what had happened three days before. The bear. And, before the bear, he remembered his thoughts about what he intended to do with Kate when he got back to the cabin. Well, no use thinking about it now. The bear had put an end to that sort of thinking for no telling how long.

"Kate?"

Kate slumped against his side, so weary she could no longer sit upright. "Yes?"

"I'm much obliged to you for taking care of me. I want you to know that." He twirled a strand of her hair in his fingers, found her ear and stroked it gently, wanting to repay her somehow. She relaxed even further and nestled against him as though she belonged there.

"You're . . . welcome . . ." she muttered, then slipped into an exhausted sleep.

Drew lay as still as possible, which wasn't hard since he'd used every ounce of strength when he touched her hair. She must have been up straight through the past nights, tending his wounds. She was a good woman. Strong. Determined. Capable. And desirable.

In spite of his throbbing leg, Drew felt a response to his thoughts and changed his train of thinking to more important matters. Firewood. Food. He'd be unable to help her for days.

How would she manage it all? There was short supply in the cabin, and the deer he'd killed . . . Where was it now? He craned his neck in both directions as far as his stiff neck would allow and caught a glimpse of antlers in the corner by the door. She'd dragged it inside to keep it safe from scavengers, dressed and butchered it herself. A deep sniff told him there was venison cooking in a pot hanging over the coals in the fireplace.

Yep, this woman was something else, all right. He'd have to get better in a hurry, before the chores involved with keeping them alive took everything she had to give. They were in dire circumstances, and it would take every bit of mountain savvy he had to get them through it alive.

Drew pulled Kate a little closer and wished he had the strength to kiss the top of her head. "We'll make it somehow, Kate," he whispered. "I promise."

CHAPTER TWELVE

Drew came to gradually, until the throbbing in his leg became more insistent than the overwhelming desire to sink back into the blackness of sleep.

"Kate?" He tried to sit up but pain drove him back onto the pallet, panting. He smelled onions. Strong.

"Don't move."

Kate's face swam before his eyes. Was she really there, or was he dreaming again? Crazy, mixed-up dreams, about Lucy and snakes and tight paper collars, and bears. Bears!

"Kate! The bear—!"

"Long dead. Now, quiet yourself. You're safe and so am I." Kate pressed her hand to his forehead and smiled. "Your fever has come down. Finally." She slumped beside him and closed her eyes.

Drew's vision cleared just enough to see her clearly. Her hair had matted in the back, her eyes were shadowed with dark circles, and her mouth seemed pale and pinched. How many hours had he lost? "Kate, how long since the bear attacked?"

"Five days ago."

"Five days! I've been unconscious for five days?"

"And a half. Hush, or I'll—" A yawn interrupted.

Drew's anger disappeared. For five days, she'd tended him. He vaguely remembered waking up once during those days, but nothing was clear enough to remember with any accuracy. There were neat bandages on his leg. His pants were gone—probably cut off him. His shirt was clean and he'd had a bath, or it felt like it, anyway. The fireplace crackled and something cooking in the pot hanging over the flames smelled awfully good. Venison.

She'd fallen asleep on his arm. He decided not to wake her. Instead, he took note of their situation and tried to decide what had to be done next. He ran his fingers through her hair and a knot in his throat almost choked him. She hadn't tended to her own needs at all, except to eat. She'd saved his life after he'd saved hers. Damn.

When Kate woke up, she heard Drew's steady, even breathing before she opened her eyes. Since the fever had broken, he was sleeping easier. Now, maybe she could clean herself up a little.

Easing away, she went to get the water buckets. She'd need plenty of water to wash away the dirt and grime she'd collected during the past five days. Outside, bundled against the cold, she stepped carefully around drifts of snow, taking care not to trigger any of the booby traps in the trees. Snow down the back of her neck would be too shocking to handle right now.

It took a long time to reach the stream. They'd had more than three feet of snow and it made for slow going. The stream had slowed noticeably and had frozen at the edges. A coating of ice reached toward the middle of the flow. Before long, it would freeze completely. Hacking chunks of ice, then melting them, would be time-consuming, hard work. They'd have to conserve water as much as possible.

She filled both buckets and lugged them back to the cabin, taking care not to slosh any of the precious water into the snow. She tiptoed inside, expecting Drew to be asleep, but he was sitting up!

"Drew! You shouldn't be sitting! Your leg will start to bleed again." She set the buckets down and went to check his wound.

"I feel like a cripple lying there." He covered himself with the blanket, shivering a little. "When you opened that door, I nearly froze to death! If that bear didn't kill me, you will with your—" He stopped when he saw her expression.

Crying softly, she snuffled into her hands. "I'm sorry. I didn't mean—"

Drew felt like pond scum. "Kate, don't cry. I didn't mean it that way. I was only funning you. Come here, woman. Come here."

Kate swiped at her eyes. Everything in the room blurred.

"Come here, woman!"

She did what he said and sat next to him on the floor. The minute she sat down, he put his arm around her shoulders and pulled her close.

"I'm sorry, Kate. I'm sorry for what I said and for not being able to help you these past days. Do you understand?"

"Whad?" She blew her nose into a rag with a loud honk.

"I'm not mad at you. I'm indebted to you more than I'll ever be able to repay."

"Are you hungry?"

"Starving. What's in the pot?"

"Venison stew. I butchered the deer and hung most of the meat outside to freeze. We'll have to hope varmints don't get to it before we need it."

More work he should've done. Damn. When she'd needed him most, he'd been out cold.

"As soon as I can move around, I'm going to make it up to you. I promise." He trailed his fingers over her face. She was beautiful even with her hair dirty and soot on her nose.

"My face is dirty."

"It's beautiful."

She honked into the rag again and dabbed at her eyes with a clean corner. "I think you're still delirious."

Drew pulled her chin up with his fingers. "You're as beautiful as any woman I've ever laid eyes on. And that's the truth."

Looking into his eyes like this was all Kate could have hoped for in her lifetime. He'd given her so much already. She knew what was about to happen and closed her eyes to let him know she was ready.

Drew's lips on hers were soft and gentle. His tongue slipping into her mouth made the fire within her burn brightly, fanned to life from an ember that had never cooled. Kate reached for him, stroked his whiskered cheek, ran her fingers through his thick hair, and hoped the kiss would last forever.

A sharp rapping at the door jerked them apart.

Drew whispered, "Get my gun and be quick about it."

Kate nodded and fetched the gun.

"Now, go to the door and wait." Drew checked the gun to be sure it was ready to fire, then nodded. "Ask who it is."

Kate trembled. It could be anyone. It could be Carson.

"Who's there?" she called in a shaky voice.

"Remington. Joshua C. I saw the smoke from your fire. If I could warm my hands a mite . . ."

Drew pulled himself around to get a better shot at the door. "Open the door."

"But, Drew, it could be a trick! It could be Carson!"

"I know Carson's voice, Kate. It isn't him. We can't deny warmth to a traveler in this weather, no matter who he might be. Open the door."

Kate lifted the bar and stood back. The heavy wooden door eased open to reveal a huge man dressed in fur. His beard, dark and matted with grease, reached halfway to his waist. His eyes peered through the tangled wreath of hair jutting from under his fur cap.

"Much obliged," Remington said, and went straight to the fire.

Kate closed the door and replaced the bar. Remington, Joshua

C., smelled worse than any other human she'd ever met, even in the saloon in Sutterfield. She tried to breathe through her mouth instead of her nose. She glanced at Drew and saw he was doing the same. Mercy! Who was this man?

Remington rubbed his face. Frost collected in his hair, beard, eyebrows and eyelashes fluttered to the floor and melted. He turned to Drew. "Hurt or ailing?"

Drew hesitated. "Bear attack. Tore up my leg pretty bad."

Remington nodded. "Got something in my pack that'll have you back on your feet in no time." He went back outside.

"Drew, what are we going to do?"

"Offer him supper. I doubt he'll stay long. He seems friendly enough."

Remington came back inside. He dropped his pack. Judging by the effort, it was plenty heavy. He rummaged inside, then pulled out a greasy package and opened it.

"Bear grease. Fix you right up."

Drew's nose wrinkled at the smell. "Are you sure about that?"

"Where I come from, ain't no doctors to take care of animal wounds. This stuff draws out the p'isins, kills some of the pain, too. What've you been using?"

"Onion plasters." Kate rubbed her hands together. They were still tender, blistered from handling the hot onions.

"Onions ain't no good atall on a bear wound. Goes too deep. A bear's claws are dirty. Here." He thrust the package at Kate. "Make a poultice and keep the leg up. You'll be walking inside of a month."

"A month!"

"Without it, you might not have a leg to walk on at all." Remington sat down at the table and peeled off his coat and two other layers of filthy clothing. The smell under his coat was indescribable.

Kate found it difficult to breathe. Remington smelled like

something long dead.

He kept stripping off clothes until he wore nothing but a shirt over long underwear. "I been walking the past twenty miles. Feels good to set a spell."

"Where's your horse?" Kate could tell that Drew was trying not to flinch at the stink emanating from the filthy man. The stench filled the room like a smoking fireplace.

"Broke a leg."

"Where you from?"

"Here and there. Right now, I'm heading for Silverton. Hear they're finding ore by the ton there." Remington looked toward the fireplace. "Got anything to eat?"

"Some stew." She went to get him a bowl, chastising herself for not being a better "wife." She stirred the pot, ladled some of the stew into a bowl, then filled another bowl for Drew. Compared to Remington, the stew smelled heavenly.

Remington rummaged in his pack again and pulled out something wrapped in what looked like stomach lining from a cow or horse. "If you wouldn't mind, ma'am, I've been hankering for a taste of fried fat for days. I'd be much obliged if you'd fry this up for me. There's enough for all of us."

Kate nodded and took the package. She placed a skillet over the coals in one corner of the fireplace, let it heat, then dumped the contents of the package into the hot skillet. It sizzled and popped. Bacon fat. Clear and white, with maggots feasting around the edges. She'd eat bark from the trees before she'd let one bite of this vile fat touch her lips. The rancid meat gave off a stench much like Remington's while it cooked. It was all Kate could do not to retch.

Remington had finished his stew and gone to stand by the fire, holding his hands out to warm them. "How long you been here?"

"About a week."

"Where you headed?"

"Laramie." Drew gave Kate a look of caution.

Kate said nothing. Obviously, Drew didn't trust the man, no matter how friendly he seemed.

"Coming from where?"

"South."

Kate flipped the fat over. If she didn't get some fresh air soon, she might keel over into the fireplace.

"You planning on being here long?"

"Just till I'm able to travel again."

"I need a horse."

"We don't have a spare."

"You're in no shape to ride."

"I will be soon."

"I have to get to Silverton." Remington dug in his coat pocket and pulled out a wad of bills. "I'll give you fifty dollars for one of your horses."

"They aren't for sale."

Remington scowled. "I could take them for nothing."

"I could kill you where you stand." Drew lifted the rifle and cocked it.

Remington laughed and dropped back into the chair. "No need for more blood being spilled, Mister . . . I don't believe I caught your name."

Drew hesitated. "Wilson."

"Mister Wilson. If it's all the same to you, I'll just be on my way once your wife has cooked my supper."

Kate used her skirts as protection against the hot skillet handle and pulled it out of the coals. "It's ready."

Remington stabbed the fat with his knife. After eating half, he dropped it back in the plate. "Much obliged. I'll be glad to leave you some."

Drew's mouth worked a little. "No thanks. You'll be hungry

come sundown."

Kate's stomach churned. She owed Drew a kiss for sparing them. If only this human stink bug would leave!

Remington replaced all the layers of grimy clothing and reached for his pack. "I hope your leg does all right. I've had worse and lived over it."

Drew didn't reply. He kept his hand on the gun.

Remington pulled his hat over his filthy, matted hair and reached for the bar on the door. "Good luck to you." He left.

Kate ran to replace the bar. She waited a full five minutes, then, unable to stand the stench any longer, she opened the door and let the icy wind swirl through the cabin. When her fingers started to smart and sting from the cold, she closed it again and put the bar firmly in place.

"I don't know which is worse." Drew pulled the blanket up around his chin. "Freezing or suffocating."

"What if he takes the horses?"

"If he does, he does. There isn't much we can do." He laid the gun down and relaxed a little for the first time since Remington had come to the door. "I doubt we could keep the horses alive much longer, anyway." He nodded, then fell asleep.

The encounter had taken more out of him than she'd expected. She covered him carefully, then added wood to the fire. She'd have to gather more in the morning, but for now, they were safe and warm, and Remington, and his foul stench, were gone.

Drew's fever rose again during the night and Kate spent fitful hours bathing his face and chest, trying to keep him cool. But the minute the cool, damp cloth touched his skin, it warmed and dried, and the fever raged on.

By morning, Kate lay exhausted at Drew's side. When he roused, she started. Drew tried to sit up but she pushed him back again.

"Be still! I'll get some broth for you."

"Broth!" He licked his dry lips. "Bring me something to chew! I had stew when Remington was here!"

"And you lost it right after he left, when your fever came back. No solid food for you yet. You were mauled by a bear, or don't you remember?"

Drew instinctively reached to the wound on his leg and winced from the pain of touching the raw places through the bandages. "Has the bleeding stopped?"

"Yes, and your fever is down some. Thank the Lord above."

"Again? How long was I out this time?"

"Only about thirteen hours." She straightened and stretched wearily. "You passed out right after—"

"Thirteen hours! But Remington just left—"

"That was yesterday afternoon. It's almost dinnertime. You're sick! Lie still and I'll get the broth."

Drew made a fist and pounded the floor beside him. "Damn. Out cold for another half a day without even knowing it." He raised his head and watched Kate getting the broth. "Did Remington steal the horses?"

"I have no idea. I haven't had time to check on them."

Drew's eyes strayed to the door. "You haven't fed them?"

Kate came back with a steaming bowl of broth. "I told you, no. I've been tending to you all night. Ranting and raving about rustlers and Carson and—"

"And what else?"

"Lucy."

"Oh." Drew averted his eyes from hers, looking embarrassed at what he might have said. "Anything else?"

"Nothing important." Kate poked the spoon at his lips until he opened his mouth. She deposited the spoonful of broth on his tongue.

"I can feed myself, Kate. I'm not a baby."

"Yes, you are. You're a two-hundred-pound baby. Open."

Drew clamped his lips together.

"I'll pour it on your face if you don't open your mouth." She held the spoon above his nose.

Grumbling, he opened his mouth, "I'd like to know what else I said."

Kate felt her cheeks pinking. "Something about 'it has to be today. This minute.' I couldn't understand everything." She set the bowl in her lap and stared at the fireplace. How could she tell him that he'd talked about making love to her? About how he couldn't wait another day?"

Drew seemed to get the idea from her silence and didn't press further. He tried to sit up, but a wave of dizziness made him give it up.

"See? What did I tell you? Finish the broth. If it stays down, you can have some venison stew later."

The aroma of the stew made Drew's mouth water hungrily. He let her help him sit up enough to drink the rest of the broth straight from the bowl, then he lay back, exhausted by the effort.

"It's time to change your bandage." Kate put the bowl and spoon away and came back carrying fresh rags. Without a word, she gently removed the old bandage, doctored the wound with more of the onions she'd used before, then bound it all up again. Never once did her eyes stray from the business at hand.

"Kate?" Drew voice was soft but compelling.

"What is it now?" She rearranged the blankets over him and took the soiled bandages to be cleaned and boiled for later use.

"I appreciate your taking care of me. A lot. I want you to know that, even when I say things I shouldn't be saying."

"I know. Rest. I'll see about the horses." She tidied up the hearth, bundled herself tightly and left Drew alone with his thoughts.

Outside, she took deep breaths of the clean, frigid air and marveled again at the beauty of snow-covered mountains. The firs and pines drooped, and juncos scratched at the ground next to their trunks, looking for seeds that weren't buried too deeply in the powdery snow. Trudging around to where the horses were sheltered under a flimsy lean-to of a barn, she hurried as much as the drifts would allow. One peek told her what she'd feared had happened. The horses were gone.

CHAPTER THIRTEEN

"Gone!" Drew's face reddened. "That no good, thieving sidewinder—"

"Now, Drew, getting yourself all in a snit isn't going to bring the horses back." Kate tried not to cry. If they'd ever had a chance to go on to Silverton, that chance had been stolen along with the horses. What would they do come spring? Even if someone did come along, they wouldn't have horses to spare, and there would be no way they could carry enough supplies to make it to Silverton walking.

Drew tried to get up from the pallet, wanting to storm around the room, ranting and raving, to get rid of the anger whirling through him like a Texas twister. The pain in his leg stopped him soon enough.

"Drew! You'll start bleeding again!" Kate hurried over to the pallet and placed her hands on his chest. He lay back, then grabbed her hand and squeezed until she cried out.

He loosened his grip. "Sorry. It isn't your fault the horses are gone."

Kate looked away. "Maybe it is."

"What? What sort of nonsense is that?"

"If I'd gone out to tend them sooner, maybe—" She gave in to the tears. "Oh, Drew, I've ruined everything." She collapsed on his chest and sobbed.

The rest of Drew's anger dissolved in Kate's tears. "Kate, hush yourself, now. You couldn't have stopped that stinking skinner from stealing the horses, even if you'd seen him do it."

Kate sat up and snuffled. "Why, of course I could've stopped him! Do you think I'm nothing more than a flower in a pot, sitting on a shelf? If I'd seen that mongrel taking our horses, I'd've grabbed that gun and blown him to kingdom come!"

Drew tried to hold in the laughter, but it proved impossible. He closed his eyes and guffawed.

Kate stuck her tightly clinched fists on her hips. "And just what, may I ask, is so golderned funny?"

"You." He wiped the tears from his eyes and reached for her.

Kate sat stiff as a ramrod.

"Aw, come on, Kate. It just struck me funny, that's all. You, standing with a gun half as big as you are, blasting a man half again bigger than I am. I—" He started laughing again.

Kate didn't know if she should punch him or kiss him. Hearing him laugh again made music in the dingy little cabin. When he reached for her again, she relaxed her spine and snuggled against him.

Drew took a deep breath and stroked her hair.

"What are we going to do?" Things had gotten to be final in a hurry. She took a deep, shuddering breath.

"We're going to stay here in this cabin until spring. Someone will come along, on their way to or from Silverton, and we'll see if we can buy a horse. If that fails, we'll send a message into Laramie to Meg McGruder and she'll send someone with horses."

Kate wondered what Meg would think about Kate and Drew spending the winter together in a mountain cabin, cut off from everybody and everything. Would she assume—

"What are you thinking about?"

Kate blushed and hid her face so he couldn't see her pinked cheeks. "About Meg."

He pulled her up to face him. "Think about me for a few minutes."

She tried to look solemn but failed. "Maybe. But only for a couple."

Drew laughed again, then pulled her mouth to his.

Kate forgot about the horses, Meg, and what would happen come spring, and thought only about the man in her arms.

Feeling bold, Kate teased Drew's lips with her tongue and felt his reaction through her fingertips, roaming through his hair and across his shoulders. When she opened her mouth wider, their tongues met and twined and caressed until she felt the awkwardness of their position and the cumbersome burden of clothing between them.

Drew wished he could will his leg to heal right now, this instant, so he could love this woman the way he'd wanted to for days. But that would have to wait. Could he stand to keep on kissing her without being able to make love to her, too? Could he stand to be in this cabin with her and not kiss her? Impossible. He'd just have to endure the discomfort. Right now, the pleasure outweighed the tightness in his loins and the pain throbbing in his leg. Right now, he could kiss her forever and be almost satisfied.

Kate fumbled with the buttons on Drew's shirt and put her hand next to his skin. It was brazen and completely inconceivable for any decent, civilized lady to do such a thing, but right now she couldn't care less. What did Drew think of her for being such a tart? From his reaction, she'd guess he didn't care, either.

Kate twisted the hair on Drew's chest around her fingers, combed through, then back again, and cried out in shock when she touched his right nipple. It felt absolutely smooth under her fingers, except for the tip, which stood up, as hard as a little pebble between her fingers.

Shame coursed through her, but Drew finished unbuttoning the shirt and pulled it out of the way.

"Kiss me."

She didn't know what he meant at first, since she'd been kissing him already. Then she let her eyes wander to his bare chest and the nipple, erect, waiting for her touch. He wanted her to kiss . . .

"Drew, I can't!" She tried to pull away, but he stopped her.

"Why not? I kissed yours. It's only fair." His mouth turned up slightly at the corners, giving him a playful look.

Kate's breath came in shudders and gasps. Drew placed his hand on the back of her neck and pressed gently. She gave in and found the nipple with her lips.

Drew sucked in a sharp breath when she circled with her tongue. He moaned deep in his throat when she flicked back and forth across the taut peak. And he almost lost control when she sucked gently.

"Kate. I want you so much."

The words bounced around in her brain. "I want you, too."

He pulled her mouth back to his while he loosened the front of her dress, then lifted her until her left breast came within reach of his lips and tongue. He teased, licked, stroked, and sucked while she moaned with pleasure, then repeated the precious agony on the other breast.

"It feels so good," she managed to whisper. "It has to be wrong."

"No, Kate. Pleasure isn't wrong. Denying pleasure when we both want it would be wrong." He went back to his task with gusto until she collapsed beside him, pulling her knees up, rolling herself into a ball.

"What's wrong? Did I hurt you?"

"No. Of course you didn't hurt me. It just felt so good I couldn't bear it any longer." She uncurled enough to mold herself around him without touching his injured leg. "How long until your leg will be well?"

He took a sluggish breath. "Too long."

"Lucy! Watch out!" Drew flailed the air and tried to get up.

Kate woke up from a deep sleep and restrained Drew the best she could. "Stop! You'll tear the wound open again!" But Drew didn't answer, and he didn't stop his ranting.

Kate could feel heat radiating from Drew like a wood stove. His fever had come back up. The wound had begun to seep blood and pus. What could she do to quiet him? He'd undo everything!

"Drew! Listen to me!"

"Snake! Look out! Rattler!"

As suddenly as he'd roused, he collapsed. Sweat rolled down his face and soaked his shirt. He was burning up. His head jerked back and forth with the dream, but Kate held him down until he lapsed into a restless sleep.

"Oh, God, what am I going to do?" Kate looked at his leg and took the bandage completely off. She'd have to pack it again and try to stop the bleeding. If only she'd been awake, she might have been able to stop him from thrashing so. The onions had helped at first, but the wound was too deep. And she had no other medicine for the infection. If she didn't do something, he'd die.

The next two days passed like a nightmare. Kate sat beside Drew constantly, bathing his face, tending the wound, which festered and reddened until she feared he'd lose his leg, if not his life. But she refused to think that either might happen. Somehow, she'd save him from the infection raging in his body. She had to.

But by sundown, the last day of October, Kate knew she'd

lost the battle. The wound refused to get better, no matter what she tried. Drew's fever had him out of his head most of the time and thrashing around with nightmares and visions. Kate couldn't hold her eyes open any longer. Her arms felt as heavy as lead. Her knees buckled every time she tried to stand.

Sobbing with exhaustion and fear and the terrible burden of defeat, Kate lay down beside Drew, unable to help him. Unable to help herself. If Drew died, she might as well die with him. In time, stranded in this cabin, she'd die anyway.

She closed her eyes and gave in to the overwhelming desire to sleep forever.

Dawn was creeping in around the door when Kate woke the next morning.

Pounding. Someone was pounding at the door.

Barely able to walk, Kate managed to stand.

"Who . . . who's there?" Her mouth was so dry, she could hardly speak. Swallowing was painful.

"Open up. It's cold out here."

Kate hesitated only a second. She couldn't deny shelter to any person in such weather, no matter who they might be. That's what Drew had said. And the thought occurred to her they might be able to help. She pulled the bar and stood back.

Snow whirled into the cabin behind the four men who came in. Kate barred the door behind them and prayed she hadn't done the wrong thing admitting them. She turned around slowly, trying to gather her composure.

The men huddled around the fireplace, warming their faces and hands. Kate knew they could be the worst sort of vermin. She reached for the gun and pointed it at them.

"I want to know who you are." She cleared her throat. The tallest of the bunch turned around.

"Now, ma'am, you ain't gonna need that firearm. We mean you no harm. We just need warmth and maybe some coffee."

"Who are you?" Her voice sounded stronger. She couldn't let them know how her knees trembled and her elbows ached from the weight of the gun.

"If you put that gun down, ma'am," the man went on, "then we'll introduce ourselves. I promise no harm will come to you."

He seemed sincere, but then he could be the biggest liar in the world. The pain in her arms made the decision for her. She lowered the gun.

"Thanks, ma'am." He squinted at her. "Don't I know you, ma'am?"

"It's quite unlikely. I'm sure I don't know you." She looked more closely at the whiskered face and worn drover's clothes. A tingle of recognition shimmied down her spine.

"I do know you. We came to your fire a while back." He took two steps toward her. "I'm Seth Brumley. Remember?"

Kate was determined not to let fear show in her face, even though she was suddenly consumed with it. "I remember."

A man who had stayed at the fire until now turned and took his hat off. Kate could see through the V of his coat that he wore a red shirt. Cole Springer.

"I don't rightly know who you are, ma'am, but the man on the floor there is Drew Kingman," the third man said.

"How do you know that?" Kate raised the gun again.

"Because I mean to kill him."

CHAPTER FOURTEEN

"Jerome Carson." Kate drew in a long breath and held it.

"So, Kingman's told you about me, has he?"

"Get out." Kate pulled back the hammer and aimed the rifle at Carson's heart.

"We're not going back out into that storm, ma'am. Just put the gun down and—"

"I'll kill you where you stand. Get out." Kate's heart threatened to explode in her chest.

"You can't kill all of us before one of my men gets to you. Let's be reasonable—"

"I don't intend to kill anyone but you." Kate pulled the gun up until it aimed straight at his eyes. "Now get out of this cabin." The weight of the gun made her elbows and shoulders scream. If he didn't give in, she'd have to surrender or kill him. And right now, killing him seemed just the thing to do.

Kate screamed and pulled the trigger when someone grabbed her from behind and jerked the gun upward. The bullets went into the ceiling.

"No! You can't kill him! I won't let you!"

She struggled against the grip of the man who held her. "Let me go, you bastard!"

"My, my, what have we here?" Jerome Carson took the gun from the man holding Kate. "A lady who uses words she shouldn't even know."

Kate glared at him. "You wouldn't know a lady if you saw

one. How dare you treat me this way? How dare you—"

"Now, let's get things straight, Missy. I couldn't care less about you or whether or not you're a lady. From the looks of you, I'd say the matter was highly debatable, but that's not our business here. I've been tracking Kingman ever since he murdered my brother, and I mean to take my revenge on him."

"Drew didn't murder your brother! He was just taking back what was rightly his!" Kate struggled against the hands biting into her arms. Carson nodded to the man to let her go.

Kate whirled around and raised one hand, intending to slap the whey out of her captor, but stopped short when she saw his face. An Indian. Tall. Dark-skinned. Eyes as black as the bottom of a well. She lowered her hand.

Carson touched her elbow. "Sit down, miss, and finish this little story of yours. As soon as you're done, I'll tell you what really happened."

Kate fled to the far side of the room. "Drew told me that his cattle were stolen by rustlers. He tracked them into Springfield but got there too late. They'd already sold his beeves and split up. He tracked your brother into Wyoming and took back the money that was his. Your brother pulled a gun and Drew shot him."

Carson started to laugh. "So that's what he told you? You must be pretty sweet on old Drew if you'd buy that tale." He frowned, as though what he'd said pained him somehow.

"Drew doesn't lie. If that's what he said happened, then that's what happened." She glanced over at Drew on the pallet. He lay so still, she panicked. "Please, God, no!"

Kate rushed to Drew's side and pressed her ear to his chest to listen. He was alive, but breathing so shallowly, she feared his heart would stop even as she listened.

"What happened to him?" Carson squatted beside her.

Kate pushed him away. "Leave him alone! He saved me from

a bear and took the slashing himself. Does that sound like a man who'd murder your brother?"

"Why, sure, if it meant getting close to a pretty little thing like you."

Kate lunged at Carson's throat with her fingers splayed, desperate to choke the life out of him. Carson grabbed her wrists and held her away from him, writhing like a snake.

"I'll kill you!" Kate screamed at him.

The Indian pulled her away. "This woman knows nothing but what she's been told."

"True." Carson studied her carefully. "Still, we can't leave her here alone. Without Kingman to—" He looked back at Drew, lying so still. "How long has he been like that?"

Kate hated having to answer, but the Indian tightened his grip on her arms until she did. "A week. What do you care?"

Carson nodded. "And you've been taking care of him and everything else during that time?"

"Of course. I'm no weakling." The Indian let go of her. She considered trying for Carson's throat again but thought better of it. The Indian might break her arms next time.

"My apologies, miss . . ."

Kate straightened her shoulders. "Mathison. Kate Mathison."

"May I ask, Miss Mathison, what you're doing here with Kingman?"

She wasn't about to tell Carson the truth. "My father is ill in Wyoming. Mr. Kingman was kind enough to offer to escort me there. We were caught by this snow. My father will be dead before I can reach him now."

Carson nodded again. "I suppose we could take you as far as Silverton. In the spring, you could head on to Wyoming. I doubt any of the miners will want to leave their claims to take you, but someone headed that direction should come by after the thaw."

Kate stepped up to Jerome Carson, who towered above her,

just as Drew did. "I wouldn't go two feet with you, Mister Carson, if my life depended on it. I'll stay with Drew as long as I have breath in my body."

"Admirable, since I'm gonna kill him."

Kate's face paled. "He's dying from the infection. You'd be shooting a dead man. Not very admirable for someone of your . . . integrity. Wouldn't you agree?" Kate held her breath. Would it work? With all her heart, she hoped so.

Carson looked around the room to test the reactions of the other men. When he looked back at Kate, her heart turned to stone.

"Miss Mathison, it really doesn't make a lot of difference to me how this man dies. I'm not out to make him suffer. I just want justice for my brother's death."

"Justice! You don't know the meaning of the word if you mean to kill a man who just wanted to recover his property. Your brother deserved to die if he'd steal a man's livelihood, then pull a gun on him."

Carson's eyes blazed at her words. "Now, Miss Mathison, I'd be a low-down skunk to hurt a woman just because she didn't have the good sense to know when to shut up, but if you say one more word about my brother, I'm gonna have to see to it that it's the last words you say."

Kate felt cold. And utterly terrified. "You're a coward, Mr. Carson, if a few words can lower you to such degradation as to threaten a woman for speaking her mind."

She lifted her chin and dared him with her eyes to say another word against her.

Carson nodded, then smiled. "You're a pistol. Kingman knew what he was doing when he teamed up with you, ma'am."

Kate didn't know what to say to that, so she turned back to Drew instead. His forehead would've cooked an egg. She went to get a cool, wet rag, then mopped his face. His breathing

148

seemed shallower than ever.

Carson addressed his men. "We'll stay the night, then head on to Silverton in the morning. Kingman's not going any place on foot, and I suspect that the lady has called it right. He'll be dead within a week."

Tears sprang to Kate's eyes when she heard her fears voiced aloud. If Drew was to survive, her only hope lay in getting shed of them and toughing out the fever and infection that still threatened his life.

Carson and his men settled into the cabin as though it belonged to them. They ate the food Kate cooked and even complimented her on how tasty it was.

Kate said as little as she could get by with and glared at Jerome Carson at every opportunity. If only she could manage to convince him of Drew's innocence . . . The other alternative was to kill him, which made her ill just to think about. She'd done lots of unsavory things in her life, but she'd never killed anyone. If the opportunity presented itself, though, she'd have to be ready. It could mean saving Drew's life, if the infection didn't kill him first.

Drew tossed and turned the first half of the night with the fever that refused to leave him. Kate never left his side. Carson and the three white men with him spread their blankets near the fire and snored loudly. The Indian sat next to the wall, eyes wide, unmoving.

Kate wondered about the Indian. How had he come to be with Carson? Didn't he sleep? What did he think about, staring into the fire that way? Drew stirred and she returned to her vigil.

Just after midnight, Drew stopped thrashing and lay deathly still. Repeatedly, Kate listened to see if his heart still beat within his chest. Exhausted beyond the limits of endurance, she resigned herself once again to the fact of Drew's death. She had no medicine to save him, and the onion plasters hadn't been strong enough. She laid her head on Drew's arm and cried softly.

Fingers on her arm. Kate sat up and stared into the eyes of the Indian, who held one finger over his mouth to tell her to be quiet. In his other hand he held something she didn't recognize.

"Put this on the wound." The Indian didn't whisper. He spoke in a voice so low it melded into the snoring of the four men on the floor.

Kate shook her head. She didn't understand.

The Indian handed her the pouch and pointed toward Drew's leg. "On the wound. It will help." Then he went back to his place by the wall and sat down again, his black eyes flashing in the flickering light of the fire.

He wanted to help Drew! Without understanding why, without caring why, Kate nodded her thanks to the Indian and undid the bandage.

The odor of putrefaction made her stomach turn over, but she bathed the wound in spite of it, then applied part of the contents of the pouch—crushed leaves she couldn't identify in the dark—to the wound. Carefully, she wound a fresh bandage around the leg.

She looked back at the Indian. He wasn't there. She saw him hunched over near the water bucket. Within a minute, he handed her a cup.

"He should drink this."

This time, when he sat down, the Indian closed his eyes to sleep.

Kate drizzled the liquid between Drew's dry, thin lips.

There was nothing left to do but wait.

Kate woke up to the noise of Carson's men getting their gear ready to leave. Disoriented for a moment, Kate was surprised to have slept since . . . well, since right after the Indian had brought her the medicine for Drew.

Immediately, she checked on Drew. He still slept fitfully, yet she sensed a change in him somehow.

"We'll be leaving directly, Miss Mathison, if you've changed your mind about going on to Silverton." Jerome Carson shouldered his rifle.

"The sooner you leave, the better, Mr. Carson." She used her most indignant "fine lady" voice. His remark about her not being a lady still had her hackles raised.

"Have it your way, then. My men are rounding up some firewood for you, and they've managed to bag a buck to give you some meat. After it's gone, you'll have to fend for yourself."

Kate stood up and straightened her wrinkled dress. She knew her dirty hair must make her look like a wild woman, but she was determined to stand up to these hooligans.

"Sir, I have fended for myself, as you so crudely put it, all of my life. I shall have no difficulty whatsoever getting along after you have gone. Now please do me the courtesy of getting out of this cabin so I can get back to work." She raised her chin just enough to be able to look down her nose at Carson and the others and hoped he couldn't see how her knees trembled beneath her skirts.

"I owe you an apology, ma'am," Carson said slowly. "I suppose even fine ladies must resort to extreme behavior when confronted with difficult circumstances."

"I appreciate your apology, Mr. Carson. Now, if you'll excuse me . . ." She turned her back on him and took a shuddering deep breath. If they didn't leave soon, Carson might notice that Drew had improved during the night. If he suspected there might be any possibility at all for recovery, he'd shoot Drew here and now. If only Drew would remain unconscious for a while longer, until they'd gone . . .

The Indian never betrayed the fact that he'd helped Drew

during the night with the medicine. In fact, the Indian never looked directly at Kate, even during her recital to Carson. At last, the gang mounted and rode away with their coat collars turned up against the sharp, bitter wind that cut to the bone. Snow had piled up against the cabin in drifts almost two feet high already. Carson would get to Silverton just in time to be snowed in. And Kate and Drew would be snowed in here. If only Drew survived.

Kate closed the door against the wind and went quickly to check Drew's fever. He didn't seem as hot as before, and she could swear he was only asleep now, and not unconscious from the sickness as before. She prepared another poultice of the healing herbs and changed the bandage.

The wound looked better, but she wouldn't have been able to say just how. It smelled better, too. The herbs had made the difference. If only she knew what they were, she might be able to gather more. She guessed from the smell of them that comfrey was part of the mixture, but she couldn't decipher the other. No mind. If it helped Drew get well, she'd be grateful for it, named or nameless.

Drew roused a bit and opened his eyes.

Waking up! She breathed a sigh of relief that it hadn't happened half an hour ago.

"Now, Drew, don't try to get up. You're powerful sick. Can you drink some of this?" She drizzled the rest of the tea the Indian had made between his lips.

Drew made a face. "Wha . . . what's this?"

"I don't know. Just drink it." She tipped the cup further this time.

"You're feeding me something and you don't know what is?" He tried to push the cup away, but didn't have the strength to do it.

"It's good medicine. Quit your bellyaching and drink it before

I slug you." Kate felt like shouting. Awake and lucid enough to be ornery. Praise the Lord and thanks be to the Indian, whatever his name might be!

Drew took two more sips, then choked. Coughing and spitting, he grimaced at the pain in his leg and reached for the bandage.

"Don't touch that!" Kate slapped at his hand the same way she'd slap a child for stealing crackers from a barrel.

"Stop hitting me, woman!" Drew pulled his hand back and collapsed on the pallet. "My head feels like someone took a hammer to it. How long have I been out?"

"I stopped counting. What difference does it make, anyway? You're going to live and that's . . . that's . . ." Saying the words aloud brought all the fear and anguish back. Kate's throat closed up as neatly as a seam on a sewing machine. She fought the tears and lost. "Oh, Drew . . ."

Drew's head still hadn't cleared, but he knew enough about what went on around him to know that Kate had worked herself into exhaustion again, because of him and this blasted wound on his leg. Damn, but it hurt. And what was that smell? Onions aplenty. And weeds of some sort. What had she used to doctor him?

"Kate, listen to me—"

She blew her nose on a rag. "Whad?"

"My tongue is so parched, it feels twice the size it oughta be. Can I have something to drink?"

"I'll get some more tea."

"No! Water will do fine. Something without a taste."

Kate smiled at him and blew her nose again. He would be all right now. As soon as she got him cleaned up and the wound doctored again, maybe there'd be time to rest a spell.

Drew improved steadily, in spite of the fussing he did constantly, and was finally able to sit up in a chair, with Kate to help keep him balanced when he walked. The wound stopped festering and healed instead, and the pain dwindled until Drew was able to take a couple of steps before having to stop.

Outside, the mountains relaxed under a thick dusting of sparkling snow, and all the mountain creatures settled down to spend the winter doing as little as possible. Kate and Drew did the same.

The meat and firewood Carson's men left for them came in handy, but before too many days had passed, even that supply ran low. Drew assumed that Kate had done it all herself, and Kate didn't bother to tell him otherwise. Now that Drew was going to live, a completely different danger faced them. Carson was in Silverton. He could still be there in the spring. Kate couldn't let Drew take her to Silverton without presenting him to Carson on a platter. Somehow, she'd have to convince Drew that she'd decided not to go on to Silverton, even though it meant giving up the silver. Drew's life was more important to her now than any amount of silver.

Chapter Fifteen

Thanksgiving already! Kate wished for some yams to go with the venison she'd fixed for dinner, but the wild onions and mushrooms would have to do. She made a pudding from flour and sugar and the one and only can of peaches they had left and watched it like a hawk while it cooked. Drew came in shivering and limped over to the fireplace to warm his hands.

"Tarnation but it's cold out there!" He flipped his hands back and forth. They were bright red from the cold in spite of his gloves.

"Dinner'll be ready soon. You need to rest a spell. I'm afraid you're going to overdo."

Drew stood up straight and gave her his "you're mothering me to death" look, which she'd learned to recognize days ago. "Kate, if you don't stop—"

"I know, I know. I'm not your mother. I just worry about you having a relapse, that's all." She took the pudding off the fire and punched it lightly in the middle with one finger to see if it was done. It was.

"I'm not going to have a relapse. Your doctoring has done the job and I'll be fit as a fiddle in no time at all. In fact, I'm feeling well enough to dance." Drew turned her around and waltzed her around the cabin, whistling an unknown tune between his teeth.

"Drew! Stop it this minute! You're liable to—"

"Liable to what? Make you smile? Make you do something

scandalous—like have fun?" He pulled her closer and hummed the next verse.

Kate laughed in spite of herself. Not so long ago, she'd feared he'd never open his eyes again, much less dance with her. She felt her cheeks flushing with the exercise and realized she'd not danced in years. Even then, she'd only danced with Ben at home, because he thought every young woman ought to know how to dance. Drew whirled her around and around. His leg kept him from being smooth, but it certainly did nothing to dampen his enthusiasm.

"Stop! I can't catch my breath!" She leaned back in his arms, safely cradled, and laughed and laughed.

Drew laughed, too, until he saw her face. Bright and alive, haloed by masses of golden hair. God, how long had it been since he'd kissed her? Too long. Somehow, during his slow recuperation, he'd not thought of it overly much—mostly when he lay still at night, listening to the regular whisper of her breathing. The days had been busy for Kate until he'd been able to help some, with gathering wood and snaring rabbits and squirrels, and all his thoughts about loving this woman proper had gotten postponed until . . . well, until he was well enough to do something about the yearning.

Kate opened her eyes and gasped. "Drew? What is it? Is your leg—"

"It's fine, Kate. I'm just fine. I was just thinking about how grateful I am to you for saving my life."

"Oh, it wasn't me, it was—" She stopped. She'd come within an inch of telling him about the Indian.

Drew grinned. "If it wasn't you, then who was it?"

Kate pressed her lips together. "Well, I guess it was me after all. I just never think of it that way, that's all."

"You should. You worked hard enough. And that medicine you used. What was it made from?"

Kate pulled free of his arms and turned back to her cooking. "Just some comfrey and other herbs. Back in Sutterfield, we had to make due with nature's bounty when there wasn't money for store-bought medicines and doctors." Her cheeks still flamed, but with the embarrassment of the lie this time.

"Well, whatever it was, it worked. And I'm hoping we don't have cause to use that medicine again while we're here."

"Me, too." She'd used it all on Drew's leg. If something else happened, she'd have no idea where to start looking for more. In fact, she doubted there'd even be comfrey in the winter in these mountains. And shepherd's purse—That had to be it! Indians carried shepherd's purse to season their food! Of course. Why hadn't she figured it out before?

Drew felt a stirring he'd suppressed for far too long. "Kate . . ."

"Not now, Drew. I have to tend to supper if we're to celebrate Thanksgiving in a proper manner."

He let out a long breath. "We've been here better than a month. It doesn't seem like that long, does it?"

It seemed much longer to Kate, but she only smiled.

Kate bustled around the cabin, getting everything ready while Drew retreated to a corner and sat there, staying out of the way. He loved watching her. It reminded him of Lucy and the short time they'd been married. Lucy never had the spunk that Kate had, and she never would have been able to see him through the bear slashing the way Kate had. Lucy had been fragile and feminine. Not that Kate wasn't feminine. She was. But in a completely different way. She could be fragile, too, he suspected, but he'd never seen that side of her. Except for when they'd slept near to one another. And he'd touched her. And kissed her. And showed her what love between a man and a woman could be like. She'd been fragile then.

"Dinner's ready!" Kate pushed a wayward tendril of hair off her cheek and took off the rag she used as an apron.

The table had been set with the best they had. Nothing fancy to be sure, but every plate and fork shone from being scrubbed to within an inch of its life. Since the accident with the bear, Kate had been meticulous about dirt in the cabin. She said she didn't want anything to hinder the healing of his leg, and her efforts must have worked, because he'd healed in record time.

They sat down opposite each other and Kate folded her hands in front of her. "I think we ought to say thanks for all our blessings, Drew."

He nodded. She closed her eyes. He watched her all during the prayer.

"Dear Heavenly Father, we want to say thanks for all the good times we've had here in these beautiful mountains." She blushed, thinking about some of those times. "Thanks for letting Drew live." She stopped to sniff and swipe at a tear. "And thanks for this food. Keep us safe and warm all winter. Amen."

"Amen." Drew reached for her hand. "This is the best Thanksgiving I've ever had, Kate."

Her face lit up like a lightning bug. "Really? It is for me, too." She brushed away another tear. "Well, let's eat it before it gets stone cold."

Drew raved over the venison roast and the onions and mushrooms, too. And when she served the pudding, Kate laughed out loud at all the noises Drew made while he ate every bite she gave him.

When he'd finished eating, Drew pushed back from the table and patted his stomach. "Best vittles in the west, Miss Mathison."

"Why, thank you very much, I'm sure, Mr. Kingman."

Kate did the dishes while Drew watched her every move, sitting on a blanket he'd spread out in front of the fireplace. And when she came to sit by the fire, he patted the floor beside him. She sat down on the blanket and timidly ducked her head, waiting. It had been so long. So terribly long.

Drew touched her hair first. And then her cheek. When his fingers coaxed her chin around, he saw tears shining in her smoky blue eyes.

"Why the tears, Kate?"

"I've missed you, Drew."

He knew what she meant. Without hesitation, he reached for her and she came into his arms willingly, aggressively, and pushed him back on the blanket. Her mouth on his. Their arms pulling closer, closer. Two heartbeats merging into one.

Drew's breathing quickened immediately. So did Kate's. His hunger for her could wait no longer.

"Kate?"

"Yes, Drew?"

He looked straight into her eyes. "Take off your clothes."

Chapter Sixteen

Slowly and carefully, she unbuttoned the dress from top to bottom. Stepped out of it. Pulled the chemise over her head. Pitched it off to the side. Gulped twice, then stepped out of her red flannel winter drawers.

Drew's face had gone quite pale. God, but she was beautiful. Never in all his life had he ever seen such a beautiful woman. Her skin, white and smooth, seemed almost transparent in the firelight. He could have sworn he could see the beating of her heart behind those perfect breasts. Even when he'd kissed them, he hadn't realized how flawless they were. He swallowed the spit that had collected in his mouth and sat up straighter.

Kate knelt in front of him.

He had no idea what she was thinking.

"Kate, I want to love you," he murmured.

She smiled ever so slightly. "It's about time."

He laughed out loud.

His clothes joined hers on the floor.

Kate took her time looking at him, just as he did with her. Washing him when he was injured, she'd been embarrassed nearly to death to see his private parts. She felt no embarrassment now. Instead, she found herself filled to overflowing with energy and excitement and something she'd never felt, except when Drew had touched her and kissed her and looked at her the way he was looking now.

Drew laid her back on the blanket and ran his hands over her body from head to toes, learning the feel of her skin, memorizing every curve and crease, stopping now and again to kiss a tender spot—the inside of her elbows, the backs of her knees, the area just below her breasts.

Kate tingled all over. His hands raised gooseflesh, then smoothed it away again. She wanted to touch him, too. Would he want her to? Of course he would. She started slowly, learning his arms and back, his chest and neck, and found out quickly that he approved of her exploration.

Drew lay down on his back, inviting her to learn more of him. She touched every part of him except that forbidden by common decency, or so she still thought of it. But he guided her hand, and she learned that, too.

Soft. Like velvet under her fingers, yet different in texture from anything she'd ever touched before. Rigid, yet smooth. Did she dare look?

Before she could decide, Drew pulled her up to kiss him. His tongue in her mouth felt as soft as the skin she'd been touching. The groans coming from him told her of his pleasure. Had she made such sounds when he'd kissed her breasts? She remembered she had, and he'd shushed her for fear she'd wake the Bridgers. How could a body experience so much pleasure and not express it? How could anything feel so wonderful?

"Look at me, Kate."

"I am, Drew." She kissed his lips, his eyes, the side of his face, his ears.

"No, Kate. I mean look at me." He tried to tell her with his eyes.

Her cheeks pinked. Her eyes seemed glued to his face. "I . . . I didn't know if you'd want me to."

"I do."

She cleared her throat as though she were about to make a speech.

"Touch me."

Her heart beat faster and faster.

"Please, Kate." He kissed her again, lightly this time.

"All right. If it'll make you happy."

He grinned. "It'll make me happy."

Anything to make him happy. She lowered her eyes and her hand at the same time. Oh. Oh, my.

He told her just how to do it. Where to touch and how. Then he lay back and groaned with the pleasure of it.

Kate found that certain strokes brought more noises from him than others. Before long, he grabbed her and kissed her harder than he'd ever kissed her before.

"Did I do something wrong, Drew?"

"No. God, no. But I can't take any more right now." He looked up at the ceiling and tried to think about gutting a pig. It worked. For the time being, anyway.

"But, Drew, you said—"

"You did exactly right, Kate," he told her. "Only now, it's your turn."

"My turn?"

He nodded and pushed her back on the blanket.

"Kate, you were raised in a saloon. Did . . ." How was he going to put this? "Did you ever lie with a man?"

"Why, certainly not!" She started to sit up but he pushed her back again.

"I didn't think so. Don't get riled up, now. I just wondered, that's all. I don't want to scare you."

"Scare me?"

"With too many new things all at once. There'll be time later on . . ."

Kate swallowed hard. What could he be thinking of? Wasn't

he going to—But she'd waited so long!

"Kate, you're pouting again." He kissed her and pulled her bottom lip into his mouth the way he'd wanted to do on the trail weeks ago.

"I thought we were . . . that is, that you were going to . . . well, I just—"

"We are."

"We are?"

"Yes. But not quite yet."

"When?"

"In a few minutes."

"But what are we going to do until then?"

Drew's smile lit up his face. "Oh, darlin', what indeed?"

He hugged her tight against him and kissed her until all she could think of was him. She hardly realized it when his right hand trailed down her back and over her bottom and around and between them.

Her eyes flew open. "Drew! What are you doing?"

"I'm going to touch you, Kate."

"There?"

"Yes, there."

"But gentlemen don't touch ladies there, even when they're married!"

"Have you ever been married, Kate?"

"No, but—"

"Then shut up and just think about how good it feels, how about it?"

"But, Drew—"

He kissed her into breathless silence before easing his hand between them again.

Kate wanted to gasp, but Drew wouldn't release her mouth. She knew she ought to stop him, but his weight pinned her to the floor. She feared that if she didn't say something soon, he'd—

Her thoughts dried up to nothing. Nothing, that is, except Drew's fingers, touching . . . caressing . . . twirling in the soft hair between her legs, inching down on either side of her private place in that crease where her legs joined her body. And then his fingers touched the area in between.

"Drew, oh—"

"Hush, Kate."

"But it's wrong, Drew. It's evil." Evil or not, it felt heavenly.

"I've told you, Kate. Pleasure isn't evil."

"It has to be, Drew. Nothing right ever felt so good."

He teased her mercilessly until she felt such longing . . . longing for . . . for what, she had no clear idea. This must be what the saloon girls in Sutterfield had begged for.

"Stop, Drew." The words were weak and indecisive, but she felt obligated to say them.

"What?" His fingers got even busier.

"Stop that."

"What? That? Or this?"

Her brain whirled. His fingers delved into the very heart of her—or that's the way it felt anyway.

If he stopped now, she'd be tempted to strangle him.

She gave up and gave in to the sensation. When he found the center of that sensation, she started making noises of her own. She arched her hips against his hand, felt the tension building, building . . .

Drew knew she was close. He wanted the first time to be mostly pleasure and very little pain. So he intensified his efforts, listening to her little sighs and groans, and hoped he was doing the right thing.

Kate thought she'd explode with the pleasure, and still it gained intensity. Stronger . . . and stronger . . . until an explosion of pleasure raced through her. She cried out, again and again, until the waves of sensation lingered in the heat of her flushed skin, nurturing her, welcoming her, just as Drew had welcomed her into his arms.

Drew held her tight until she relaxed, then found her mouth with his. Her lips lay slack at first, then responded until she kissed him back with all the fervor he'd come to expect from her.

"Feel good?" He stroked one breast lovingly.

"Oh, Drew, now I know what they begged for."

"What?"

"Never mind. It was wonderful. Somehow, though, I need something . . . more."

Drew smiled. "I know what it is, Kate."

"You do?"

"Yes. But it will hurt a little."

"That's all right. What is it?"

"I'll show you."

Drew got up on his knees above her. "Touch me again, Kate." She did as he asked.

He guided her hand. She guided him. Her eyes came open when she realized what was happening. She put her arms around him and pulled him down to her.

He eased into her as far as he could.

"Drew, I love you," she whispered.

The pain came as a surprise, but it passed quickly.

Kate moved with Drew, marveling at how mistaken she'd been before. She'd thought her body had been as close to Drew's as it was possible to be, but it was nothing like this. Two bodies. Joined. So close they seemed more like one body than two.

"Drew, it's a miracle," she murmured.

He didn't answer. It took all his concentration, but he

determined to make this first time the best it could possibly be. Before long, though, he thought of only one thing. The woman in his arms. The woman he'd become a part of. The woman he'd grown to love.

"Kate, I'm sorry—"

"Sorry? I don't understand." She held him tighter.

"I can't . . . wait . . . any longer . . ."

His body arched and Kate held him closer, fearing he was sick or in pain or dying. The sounds he made were like an animal in a way. What on earth had she done? What was happening to him? Oh, God, please . . .

He collapsed on top of her. From the way he breathed, it seemed he'd run two miles straight without stopping.

"Drew, are you all right? Drew?"

"I'm fine, darlin'."

"You are?" Relief flooded through her. "Are you sure?"

He raised up on his elbows just enough to look into her eyes. "I'm sure. Did it hurt too much?"

"Not much. Was it supposed to?"

He laughed and rolled back onto the blanket. "I don't think so. It was my first time in a way, too."

Kate shivered suddenly. She grabbed the edge of the blanket and pulled it around her, then touched Drew's arm. More than ever, she longed to be near him. What they'd done . . .

Drew recognized the doubts creeping into her expression and hugged her soundly. "Don't you be feeling guilty, now, you hear?"

"Of course I feel guilty. Men and women aren't supposed to do such things when they aren't married." Shame tormented her already.

Drew didn't know exactly how he was going to handle this, but he had to help her over the guilt—or she'd not want to make love again. It could be a much colder winter than they already faced if she made up her mind that way.

"Kate, we're in a different situation here on this mountain the way we are."

"How do you mean?"

"We're stuck here for the winter. Just you and me. We've had to pretend we're husband and wife on this trip, and now we're living here together, just as a husband and wife would in the same situation."

"I suppose."

"And it's only natural that we'd want to do the things that a husband and wife would do in this same situation, don't you agree?"

"I suppose."

What was she thinking? He couldn't tell.

"So there's no reason for you to be feeling guilty about doing what comes naturally." To a man and a woman in love.

Kate thought it over. If she agreed, then he'd want to make love to her again. Hopefully soon. If she disagreed, then she'd have to put her foot down and say, "No more hanky panky in this cabin for the rest of the winter." She shivered just to think about it. No, the best thing to do was to agree and deal with the guilt later. After all, who was to know what they'd done but the two of them? That sounded good to her.

"I see your point, Drew. And I think you're right. I have just one more question."

Drew held his breath a little. "What is it, Kate?"

"How long before we can do it again?"

Drew laughed until tears rolled from his eyes.

"Give me about ten more minutes, darlin'. Can you wait that long?"

"I expect I can." She didn't have to wait ten minutes to kiss him again, though.

CHAPTER SEVENTEEN

Drew woke up slowly, stretched, scratched the top of his head, rolled over, and reached for Kate. Who wasn't there. He opened his eyes, but heard her before he spied where she was.

Fully dressed, boiling something in a pot over the fireplace. Humming something to herself. Looking absolutely scrumptious.

Drew couldn't remember sleeping better in his life than he had last night. He smiled, remembering all they'd done together. What a woman!

"Kate?" He waited for her to turn around. "Come back to bed?" He patted the blanket beside him.

Kate's expression never changed. "Why of course I'm not coming back to bed! There's work to be done and you know it. There's meat to be tended and stew to cook and clothes to mend and a thousand other chores that have been sliding around this place, thanks to you. Now, leave me be. I'm busy." She turned back to the kettle.

Stunned to the bone, Drew ran the little speech through his sleepy mind again. Had he dreamed making love to her the night before? Three times? Had she forgotten? Impossible. No one could forget a night like the one they'd shared. And then it hit him.

This was Kate's way of maintaining her dignity. Avoiding guilt. That had to be it. All right, then, they'd do it her way. He got up from the blanket and stood there until she turned around.

Kate yelped at the sight of him and whirled back around.

"Drew! Put some clothes on! Lawsy, you startled me to death!" Her cheeks blushed crimson and she patted them nervously. "The very idea, standing na-naked . . . that way. In front of a lady. You ought to be ashamed of yourself."

"Yes, ma'am." He was right. During the day, they'd play this little game, which could be called the cowboy and the lady. At night? He'd have to wait and see what happened tonight. Would she come to him willingly? Would he have to woo the fine lady to his bed again? Once the sun went down, would she drop this little game and let him ravish her body the way he had last night? He smiled. This little game might prove to be fun.

He pulled on his britches and shirt and reached for his coat and hat. "I'm going out to see what sort of game I can scare up."

"See to that venison first." Her tone suggested no nonsense would be tolerated.

"Yes, ma'am."

Kate turned to look at him and saw a silly grin. She gave him a tight little smile in return and shivered when he opened the door. The wind had died during the night, but the cold still swarmed in whenever it found an opening.

She stood stock still until the door closed, then collapsed into a chair.

"Oh, dear Lord, what have I done?" She reached for the rag in her pocket and blew her nose. Well, what was done was done. Drew hadn't questioned her brusque manner. Just the opposite. He seemed positively amused by it. Well, amused or not, she had no intention of behaving any other way except like a proper lady around him. Unlike last night.

Last night!

She closed her eyes, remembering. Brazen, that's what her behavior had been. Brazen and lustful. Outrageous. Inexcusable. Unforgivable. Uncontrollable.

Her shoulders slumped, then trembled with the sobs that overwhelmed her. So this was what it felt like to be in love. To be so wrapped up in another human being that his breath became her breath. His heartbeat her heartbeat. His body her body. Delicious. Fantastic. Indescribable. Exquisite. There weren't enough words to describe the pleasure he'd given her. And she'd given him pleasure, too. No doubt about that. But men didn't link pleasure with love, did they? Of course they didn't. Only women made that mistake. Only a brazen hussy would allow herself to be pleasured by a man and not fall in love with him.

But she had fallen in love with him. Did that mean she wasn't a hussy? Did that excuse her for inexcusable behavior? Did all this mean she had to choose between being virtuous—or as virtuous as possible after what had happened—and letting him make love to her again?

"Oh, God, help me decide what to do," she blubbered, and blew her nose again. "I love him. God help me, but I do." She snuffled her way back to the pot of stew bubbling over the fire and gave it a vigorous stir.

What would she do tonight when it was time to go to bed? Sleep across the cabin from him? Unthinkable. Let him kiss her good-night—but nothing more? Torture. Lie next to him and love him the way they'd loved each other last night—but say nothing?

If she did what she wanted to do—without thought to propriety and honor and virtue—there'd be no decision to make. She'd go to him. Willingly. Joyously. Gratefully.

Ten hours until dark. What would she do?

Drew came in two hours later, shivering and limping badly.

"Drew, what happened?" Did you hurt your leg again?" *Not*

that! Please, not that! She ran to help him over to the fire.

"Fell down. Like a greenhorn kid. Ow! Watch it, woman! That hurts."

Kate stuck her lip out. "I just wanted to help, that's all. If that's the way you feel about it, I'll just let you tend to your injuries by yourself." She stalked across the room and fiddled with the mending she'd been doing.

Drew felt like a reprobate. Why did she have to be so damned sensitive all the time? "Kate, I'm sorry. I didn't mean to snap at you. My leg is just throbbing to beat all. Could you help me with my boot? Please?"

Kate looked over her shoulder at him. He was trying to be nice. She had to give him that. "All right. I guess I should have known. I'm sorry, too." She straddled his leg with her back to him and gripped the boot.

Drew was startled beyond words. She must have helped her brother with his boots in this manner. Well, as long as she was willing . . .

He put his other foot on her backside and pushed. She and the boot came off his leg.

Kate turned around to set the boot beside his chair, saw his eyes, and realized what she'd done. "I . . . that is, I . . . always before . . . Ben . . . I—"

"It's all right, Kate. I understand." He tried not to smile, but it was just too funny. He burst out laughing.

"Well, I never!" Kate stomped over to the kettle and gave it such a stir that it sloshed into the fire and hissed in the red coals. Her face burned along with the stew.

"Come here, Kate." Drew swiped at the tears in his eyes.

"What for?"

He stopped laughing. "Because I said so, that's why."

"And who are you to be telling me what to do?" She refused to look at him. Instead of acting like a proper lady after last night's debauchery, she'd gone and compromised herself again. Shameful!

"I'm the one whose life you saved, that's who. Now come here."

His reasoning didn't make any sense, but she supposed it didn't matter. She took her time tasting the stew, then walked carefully toward him, taking care not to stand too close.

"What do you want, Drew?"

His look of consternation melted into one of undeniable desire. "You. I want you."

"I fail to understand—"

"Like hell you do. Come here, woman."

He reached for her.

She tried to run.

He caught her.

She struggled.

He kissed her.

She melted into his arms. And kissed him back.

He lowered her to the floor.

"Drew, we can't."

"Why not?"

"Because, we just . . . just . . . can't . . ."

Nuzzling her neck the way he did robbed her of thought. She gave in and tumbled with him on the floor, mouth to mouth, body to body, until he knocked his head against the leg of a chair.

"Tarnation!"

Kate used it as an excuse to escape. "See there? What did I tell you? Now, let me get back to my work and see to it that you do the same."

Drew propped himself on one elbow and rubbed the sore spot on his head. "Yes, ma'am."

Well, that answered his question. Tonight, when they got

ready for bed, she'd be there for him. He'd be ready and waiting.

Chapter Eighteen

Dusk.

Kate's heart hammered in her chest. Her palms required constant drying on her rag apron. Her knees felt weak and trembly. Drew got up from the table and handed her his empty plate.

"Mighty good stew, Miss Mathison."

"Thank you, Mr. Kingman."

How had they gotten back to surnames again? she wondered suddenly. It had happened when Drew came in from dressing the deer. That quaint little smile of his preceded the formal name. A joke?

Drew stretched, yawned, and scratched his stomach. "I'm really bushed. Think I'll turn in early tonight."

Kate's mouth dried up to dust. "Early?" Was he not even going to suggest—

"You look kind of tired, too. Why don't you turn in early tonight? Probably got a passel of chores to take care of tomorrow."

"Chores? Oh, yes. Chores. Always a passel of chores to do."

Drew unbuttoned his shirt so slowly that Kate was tempted to rush over and do it for him. Two. Three. Why was he being so meticulous about the buttons? Four. Five. The shirt came off his muscular arms, slid down his wide back, and dropped to the floor. His nipples stood straight out, just as they had that night she'd . . . kissed them.

Drew's smile widened.

Kate took a shuddering breath and tried to look away, but he'd started to undo the top of his britches now. A lady would look away, she told herself, and kept right on watching.

The buttons. One. Two. Why did he take such pains? Three. His thumbs stuck under the edge. Pushing. Down. Over his slim hips, covered with a fine sprinkling of blond hair. He wasn't wearing any drawers. Under the britches, which he'd pulled on this morning, he was as naked as a baby bird freshly hatched.

Drew's lips twitched a little.

Kate finally made herself look away. A lady didn't watch a gentleman undress to the altogether! She looked back.

Silhouetted against the light of the fireplace. All his clothes piled in the floor. The look on his face. The desire in his eyes.

Kate unbuttoned her dress. Slowly. One. Two.

Drew waited. His smile gone now. His eyes following every button.

Three. Four. She took two steps toward him. Five. Six. Another step. Seven. Another. Eight.

He helped her ease the dress over her shoulders and down her arms. His hands on her waist warmed already feverish skin. The dress joined the pile of clothes on the floor.

One finger on his chest.

Lips on lips.

Skin against skin.

With a sigh, they settled down for a night of love and pleasure.

CHAPTER NINETEEN

"A Christmas tree?"

"Yes, Drew, a Christmas tree."

"But we don't have anything to decorate it with."

"You'd be surprised." Kate flopped down in his lap and twirled one finger around his ear. She knew just what sort of persuasion to use to get him to give in to this particular whim. During the past month, she'd become an expert at getting just about anything from this wonderful man with the talented fingers, mouth, and body.

Drew squirmed.

Kate circled the same ear with her tongue.

Drew squirmed harder. "Kate, you know what that does to me."

"I know." Her breath on his ear provided the final persuasion.

"All right! If you don't want to forget about your silly Christmas tree and everything else you intended to do this afternoon, you'd best stop that."

Kate sat up straight. "Then you'll get me a tree?"

Drew couldn't help smiling and nodding. How could he resist a face like that? How could he resist her, when she could drive him absolutely crazy with her teeth and tongue when she put her mind to it?

It was amazing, really. Kate had taken to sex the way a duck takes to water. After the first couple of nights, she'd loosened up and talked to him while they made love. And once she started talking, she couldn't stop. She told him exactly what felt good and what didn't. And he told her, too. And now, after a month of practice, they had the pleasuring down pat.

"Drew, you aren't answering me." Kate's mouth straightened into a line. "What are you thinking about if not about my tree?" She knew the answer before she'd asked the question, but she liked to tease him.

"This." He sucked at her lips until he had the bottom one—his favorite—in his mouth. It didn't take a lot of work to get her to kiss back. What a woman!

Kate pushed back on his chest and let out a sigh. "Drew, I really do want that Christmas tree. Please?"

He made her wait just long enough to get one more kiss before he gave in. "All right. How tall do you want this tree to be?"

"About as tall as you."

"That shouldn't be too hard to find." He nibbled on her neck.

"Drew . . ."

"Hmmmmm?"

"The tree?"

"What tree?"

"Drew!"

"All right!" He planted one last peck of a kiss on her pursed lips and headed for the door. "I guess you know I'm gonna freeze getting this dadburned tree for you."

"I'll warm you up when you get back."

His smile stretched across his face. "Promise?"

"Cross my heart." She trailed her fingers across her chest, neatly outlining her breasts.

Drew took two quick steps back toward her.

"Drew!" She pointed toward the door. "First the tree."

"Yes, ma'am."

After he'd gone, Kate burst out laughing. Never in all her borned days had she imagined life could be so downright wonderful! As far as she was concerned, spring could never come at all, and she'd be content to stay right here in this cabin with Drew for the rest of her days.

She hugged herself with sheer glee. And then she thought about Silverton.

They'd have to leave the cabin in another two or three months, depending on the snows, and then would come the task of convincing Drew that she didn't want to go on to Silverton after all. After all she'd put him through, he'd be madder than a wet hen when she told him, but it had to be done.

Carson could still be in Silverton. He believed Drew was dead. When he saw he was alive, Carson would kill him on sight, for sure. Tears stung Kate's eyes and her chest hurt with the pressure that came when she thought about anything in the world hurting Drew.

No. She wouldn't let anything happen to Drew if she could help it. She'd insist they go back to Laramie. She'd tell him she'd lied about the silver mine and that her pa really was dying and she knew for a fact he'd already died and that they had no business going any farther for no good cause. He'd be furious with her, and might never speak to her again. But he'd be alive, and that's all that mattered.

A wave of dizziness made Kate grab for the edge of the table to steady herself. Now where had that come from? It passed soon enough. But then her stomach turned over, for no reason at all, and she rushed to the front door, thinking she would puke up her breakfast for sure, but nothing happened, so she shut the door, shivering, thinking she must be coming down with the epizooty.

Drew got back a while later and found Kate breathing steam

from a bowl of hot water.

"What's the matter? Head stopped up?"

"Sort of." She took another deep breath, then took the bowl to the sideboard. "I'm fine." She looked around and her face fell to match several strands of limp, damp hair trailing around her cheeks. "Didn't you get a tree?"

"Of course I got a tree. Did you think I'd dare come back without one?"

"Well, then, where is it?"

"Outside. I figured I'd try to shake more of the snow off before I brought it in."

Kate hurried to the door to look, then thought better of it. If she really was getting sick, it wouldn't do at all to get her wet head out in the cold wind. She watched Drew warming himself by the fire instead. "How big is it?"

" 'Bout as big as me."

"Is it a nice one? Even and full?"

"Sorta. You may not like it." Drew peeked over his shoulder at her and suppressed a smile.

Kate stuck her hands on her hips. "Drew Kingman, you're funnin' me!"

"Who, me? Funnin' you? Whatever for?" He couldn't hide the smile this time.

Without warning, Kate burst into tears and hid her face in her hands.

Drew couldn't believe it. "Aw, now, Kate, don't cry. I didn't mean to—"

Kate wanted to stop crying, but couldn't. So she let Drew gather her into his arms and rock her like a baby while the tears continued to pour from her eyes like a waterfall.

"I . . . I'm . . . s-sorry . . ." She buried her face in his shirt until she'd made a wet spot the size of a saucer.

Drew stroked her hair and made soothing noises until she

calmed down. "I didn't mean it, Kate, honest I didn't."

"Didn't mean whad?" she asked, dabbing at her nose with a rag from her pocket.

"Whatever it was that set you off. I don't know. Just . . . whatever. I'm sorry."

Come to think of it, Kate couldn't really say what it was that had set her off, either. She'd just started to cry, apparently for no good reason. Drew must think of her as a purely flighty female to do such a foolish thing.

"It's all right, Drew. I'm fine now. Do you want to bring the tree in now so I can see it, or should we play the game a while longer first?" She blew her nose loudly, then stuffed the rag back in her pocket.

"No more games, Kate." He kissed her lips, which were salty from the tears. "Hide your eyes."

"Hide my eyes? You promised no more games, remember?"

"Please?" His boyish grin melted her protests and she obliged.

Kate shivered when the wind from the open door hit her, but she kept her eyes resolutely shut as she'd promised. Far be it from her to break a promise to Drew Kingman. The rustle of branches and the smell of pine filled the room.

"Open your eyes."

She did and gasped with pleasure. "Drew, it's the most beautiful Christmas tree I've ever seen! Where did you find it?" She felt the thick, deep green branches and took deep breaths to take in as much of the tantalizing odor as possible. How could they have celebrated Christmas without a tree?

"Since we're stuck here on a mountain, it was really hard to find a tree, but I kept looking until I found one."

More teasing. Kate felt like bursting into tears again, but she didn't. He just wanted to make her laugh. So why did she feel like crying?

Drew saw the look on her face. "Kate? Don't tell me—"

Kate turned away.

Drew felt helpless. What was happening? Kate had never minded being teased before. She was getting sick. That must be it. It had her all out of kilter.

"Kate, I think you must be coming down with something. Why don't you lie down for a spell? I'll set the tree up and we'll decorate it later."

Kate snuffled a reply and went to lie down, curled into a tight little ball with her knees almost under her chin. Drew covered her with a blanket, then eased around the room, trying not to make any noise.

Damn. Of all the mean things to happen at Christmas, when they ought to be celebrating and having fun and making love from daylight to dark. Well, maybe she'd be well by New Year's. They'd celebrate then.

CHAPTER TWENTY

Kate woke up two hours later feeling fine. Embarrassment over her earlier behavior made it difficult to approach Drew at first, but he was so understanding, they forgot all about it and threw themselves into the merriment of decorating the tree.

Drew had wedged the trunk of the tree with three logs notched together to make a base. The tree stood near the front door, far enough away from the fireplace to avoid sparks or flying embers catching the decorations on fire. The last thing they needed, with the weather so cold, was to be left without shelter.

Kate used strips of cloth and tied bows all over the branches. Drew found a bush loaded with red berries and Kate sewed them together with her last bit of thread to make a garland. She'd retrieve the thread after they took down the tree. No one could call it fancy, but Kate loved it just the same.

"Isn't it beautiful?" She leaned back against him and gazed dreamy-eyed at their creation.

"Considering where we are and the limitations of our supplies, I have to say it's a mighty handsome tree at that." He stroked her arm, then squeezed one breast lovingly.

Kate closed her eyes and savored the sensations running through her like warm honey on a summer day. "That feels good," she murmured.

Drew kissed her neck and the tender skin behind her ear. He knew she loved being kissed in that particular place as much as he did. The now-familiar sounds coming from her assured him his attentions were appreciated. He turned her around and kissed her lips five or six times lightly before giving in to the impatience of his desire. He found her equally impatient. That's all it took.

"Drew, oh, Drew, love me, love me . . ."

Her words doubled the flames inside him. They grappled with clothing until no barrier remained between them. Lips and hands stroked, caressed, teased, until both were breathless.

Drew couldn't wait any longer. He found her ready.

"Hold me." Kate craved the intimacy they'd found more than food or water. Having him close fed her as no meat or drink could ever do.

Drew entered her with ease and pulled her body as close to his as possible. He'd never get enough of this woman. If he lived to be a hundred, he'd want to hold her, love her, give her pleasure, and be pleasured in return.

When they lay exhausted in each other's arms, eyes closed, bodies damp and cooling, Drew pulled Kate close again, wanting the wonder of loving her to go on and on. With winter raging outside and months ahead of them before spring, there was no need to think about anything other than this moment together.

A twinge of guilt made him sigh. If only he didn't have Carson to think about . . .

Christmas morning brought the first sunshine in days. Kate almost squealed to see it. They'd had nothing but snow and icy wind for weeks, or what seemed like weeks. Drew declared it the worst winter in a decade. Kate secretly thanked the Lord for extending the time they would have together. Each drift meant a few more hours or days before they could travel. A bit more time before the dreamer had to return to the reality of the real world—and bid the dream good-bye.

Drew waited as long as he could stand it before he pulled a small chest from behind the woodpile and set it down in front of Kate.

"Where did this come from?"

"I found it in the stock shed after that sidewinder stole our horses. When I saw what was in it, I decided to save it." He leaned over and kissed her sweetly. "Merry Christmas, Miss Mathison." He opened the lid slowly.

Kate's cheeks, flushed from the kiss and the excitement, paled a bit, then hugged him tightly.

"Wool! And thread! And muslin! Drew, where did it all come from?" She pulled each item from the chest, examined it lovingly, then set it aside, looking to see what other treasures remained. "Scissors! There's everything here I need to sew anything I want! I can make a new dress that isn't so tight around my—That is, that won't squeeze the breath out of me all the time."

"I kind of figured that might be your first thought." Drew loved the way she stroked the muslin. As rough as the material was, she caressed it as though it were satin or velvet.

"You think Remington left it?"

"Yep. Maybe as payment for the horses."

Kate hugged the materials to her bosom. "What a kind man."

"He was a stinking horse thief. But leaving the chest was a decent gesture, I suppose."

Kate felt a lump form in her throat. "A horse thief, yes. And stinky, without a doubt. But there was good in that man, too. This is the proof."

"I reckon."

She sniffed, reaching for the rag in her pocket. "He couldn't have chosen a more needed gift. Only yesterday, I used the last of the thread making those berry garlands. Now I won't have to wash and save that thread after Christmas. There's enough

thread here to make half a dozen dresses and shirts." She burst
into tears.

Drew let out a long sigh. "Now what?"

"It was so nice of him. He took the horses, but he left the
chest . . ." She stopped to blow her nose. "I was glad he took
them."

"Why in tarnation would you be glad?" This woman got
harder to understand by the minute.

"Because I didn't know how I was going to keep them fed
and watered through the winter, that's why. We couldn't very
well bring them in the cabin and feed them rabbit stew, could
we? He took a powerful burden off my shoulders. I can't help
being grateful for that."

"When you look at it that way, I guess you're right."

"There's even some yarn for crocheting." She could still make
a scarf for Drew—her Christmas gift to him. It wouldn't take
her two days to finish it. She gathered everything back into the
chest and closed the lid. It was heavier than she expected when
she picked it up. For some reason, her back seemed to be
bothering her some the last few days. Must be about time for
her monthly.

Kate put the chest away. Before leaving it, she trailed her
fingers along the top, considering all the possibilities it
contained. If only she'd had the wool in time to make the scarf
so she could've given it to him now. Lawsy! She hadn't even
thanked him for the chest!

"Drew!"

He swiveled from stoking the fire and turned around just in
time to catch her. She plastered herself against him with her
mouth on his. Her tongue on his lips made his insides burn as
brightly as the pine stump he'd just put into the fireplace.

"Mercy, woman. What was that for?"

"Thank you. For the most wonderful Christmas present I

ever received." She almost told him she loved him, but the words stuck in her throat. If Drew knew she loved him, his attentions to her might melt like snow under the sun's rays. She certainly didn't want that to happen.

Drew held her and rubbed little circles on her back. The best present she'd ever had. If she were his wife, he'd give her every pretty thing he could afford to buy. Velvet and satin for dresses. Feathers for her hair if she wanted them. Cameos and brooches and so much material and yarn she'd never run out.

He stiffened in her arms.

"What's wrong?"

He deliberately relaxed his muscles and nuzzled the satiny skin of her throat. "Nothing. Just a twinge from my leg."

He bit his lip and swallowed the words. How could he tell Kate he'd come to love her when Carson was intent on killing him on sight? He had no business raising her hopes with pretty words—no matter how true those words had become—then leave her later, crying over his dead body. Of course, that might not happen. He might be able to out-draw Carson, but he had the suspicion Carson wouldn't give him the chance to shoot first. Neither of them would be able to pull the trigger to kill the other in a fair fight. They'd been friends too long for that to ever happen.

"Drew?" Worry rose in her until she felt it squeezing her heart.

He looked straight into her eyes. "I just wanted to say Merry Christmas again. I'm glad you like the sewing pretties."

"I love them." *But not as much as I love you,* she wanted to say. She'd give up everything she owned to hear him say those words to her. She'd never hear them from another man, and even if she did, they'd mean nothing.

Drew pulled her tight against him and buried his face in her hair. Sweet, soft, fragrant. Like the woman he held. The woman he loved. God, but it hurt. He'd never felt this way about Lucy. He'd been fond of her. He even loved her a little, he supposed. But never had he lost his senses around her the way he did with Kate. Never before had he suffered from being away from her the way he did when he had to leave Kate to fetch water or hunt for game. Every minute away from Kate was like taking a whipping in the woodshed.

Kate wanted to scream at the top of her lungs, "I love you!" Then she wanted to whisper the words into his ear and hear them whispered into her own. She wanted to climb to the top of this mountain and shout to the world that a miracle had happened. She loved this man and he loved her in return! Unbelievable! Remarkable! Marvelous! Wondrous! Miraculous!

Drew pulled her down on the floor and reached for their sleeping blankets with one hand.

"Again?" Kate mumbled against his lips.

"Again." Drew flipped the buttons loose with ease, having had sufficient practice by now, and eased the dress down over her shoulders. He kissed her throat, her chest, the rise of each breast, then sucked gently at her nipples until she mewed her arousal in soft tones.

Kate wanted to touch him, too, but he quieted her roaming hands, insisting on doing the loving while she lay there, drowning in pleasure and desire.

Drew wanted to kiss all of her. He'd never thought of such a thing with Lucy. She would've slapped his face and called him an ugly name. Would Kate react with indignation? Was it worth taking a chance?

Kate felt the dress leaving her body and reached again for Drew's shirt and helped him out of his clothes. Cold air, gathered on the floor, made her shiver a little, but it didn't last long. Drew's hands warmed her as no fire could ever do. His fingers, laced in her hair, rubbing over her breasts, gave her shivers of a different kind as he traced lower, probing, teasing, driving her crazy. Drew had a power over her she couldn't define. Drunk on love, she decided. Intoxicated and wanton.

His lips followed his fingers to each breast, then back to her lips before he spread wet kisses over her stomach. And lower. Still lower.

"Drew?" What was he doing? Inching away from her and down, stretching out until . . . "Drew!"

"I'll stop if you want me to. Just say the word." He kissed her knees, behind her knees. The tops of her thighs. The soft skin inside her thighs.

Kate lay stiff for a moment, frightened to death she'd consented to an act that would send her to hell for sure. But the feelings tingling through her weren't devilish at all. They were heavenly. How could she possibly tell him to stop when—She stiffened again. His lips had inched up, up, until he was kissing her belly button. His tongue flipped in and around until she quivered all over. Then . . . What should she do?

Drew hesitated, wondering if she'd back out. He hoped with all his heart she wouldn't. Kissing the tender skin around her naval, he made up his mind. She could always say no.

Kate held her breath. Was he actually going to do what she thought he was thinking about doing? Kiss her . . . there? He couldn't possibly be . . . thinking about . . . about . . . Her thoughts dried up. Her brain was unable suddenly to think about anything but the exquisite sensations she'd never imagined, even in her wildest dreams. Nothing else mattered as the tension grew, and got stronger until she arched her back and cried out his name.

Drew stayed with her until she relaxed, then he couldn't bear it any longer. He entered her, desperate for release of the glorious, incredible, passionate desire threatening to explode within him. With each thrust, he carried them higher, until Kate pulled him against her, an avalanche sweeping everything away, shuddering, rushing into the depths of love they formed with their joined bodies. Trembling, gasping, they clung to each other, kissing, touching, loving.

Kate couldn't hold him close enough, kiss him hard enough, feel enough of his bare skin against hers. How could she go on living without him? Why would she want to?

Drew hated to let her go. Hated the thought of leaving her in Silverton with her father and running in front of his best friend's gun. He despised the image in his mind of arriving home in Texas. An empty house. Empty pastures. An empty man without Kate. How could he leave her? But how could he stay, endangering her life? Would there be life without her?

Whispering so softly she wouldn't be able to hear, Drew breathed, "I love you."

CHAPTER TWENTY-ONE

Kate closed her eyes and breathed deeply of the almost-warm breeze ruffling her hair and tickling her cheeks. Could spring actually be coming? Was there anything she could do to stop it?

Drew chopped wood with such vigor she thought he'd bust a gut doing it. Love washed through her like the rain they'd had last night. Rain! But then it was April and time for the snows to melt, time for the birds to come back, time for new life.

Kate dropped one hand to her swelling belly. Before long, she wouldn't be able to conceal her condition. Drew would surely notice soon.

"Won't be needing too much more of this," Drew called, burying the axe in the chopping block. Standing there without his coat, mopping his brow with one sleeve of a flannel shirt, he smiled and broke her heart again.

Soon they'd be heading for Silverton. Even without the horses, they could walk until they happened on a mining town where some horses could be bought.

The image of Carson's face barged into Kate's thoughts for the first time in weeks. Might as well be the devil himself, Kate thought bitterly. As long as they had to walk to Silverton, she'd carry the hope that Carson would be gone before they arrived.

Drew started for the cabin, then stopped, raised one hand to shade his eyes from the blessedly warm sun, and shook his head. "Well, I'll be damned."

Kate tried to see what he was looking at. "What is it, Drew?"

"Would you believe a horse thief?"

Kate drew in a sharp breath when she saw the horseman approaching from the south.

"Hello, the house!" Remington shouted. He was leading two horses and a mule.

Drew pulled the axe from the block and leaned on the handle. He motioned for Kate to go back in the cabin.

"But, Drew—"

Remington pulled up short. "I'm sorry about taking your horses, Kingman."

"And?" Drew wasn't about to give him any slack.

"I've brought them back."

Drew stood up straighter. "Those aren't the horses you stole, Remington."

The skinner led the line of animals closer and tied his horse to a low tree limb. "You're right about that. One of your horses took sick and died about a week after I got to Silverton. The other one I traded. I figured I ought to bring you sound horseflesh after taking them the way I did."

Drew glanced over at Kate. Kate raised her eyebrows in a silent question.

Remington stared hard at Drew. "I knew your missus there would be hard pressed to feed and water your stock with you laid up and all. In a way, you might say I did us both a favor by taking 'em."

Kate went to stand beside Drew. "We're much obliged to you."

Drew glared at her. "Obliged!"

"For bringing the horses back. You were right about it being a burden to me. I'm much obliged to you for the thought." She reached for Drew's hand and found it rigid, but his fingers relaxed after a squeeze or two.

"I suppose I should thank you, too," Drew said begrudgingly.

"But it's hard to thank a man for stealing." He felt Kate nudge him in the ribs. "I'm obliged to you for bringing them back."

Remington's face lit up as much as the grime caked on his cheeks and in his beard would allow. "I was hoping you'd see it as trading. I'm guessing you found those pretties I left for you."

"It was a real blessing to find all you left for us. Thank you." Kate hated what she had to do next. "Would you be thinking of staying a spell with us, Mr. Remington?"

"Thanky, ma'am, but I'd best be getting on down the mountain. I appreciate the offer, though." He grinned, exposing toothless gums.

Kate thought about asking where he'd lost his teeth, but decided she didn't want to know.

Drew hesitated, then offered to shake Remington's hand.

Remington rubbed his hand on his filthy clothes, which did nothing to clean the grime caked between his fingers, and shook Drew's hand heartily.

Drew pulled his hand back, and Kate could see he just barely resisted the temptation to rub it on his britches. He gripped the handle of the axe instead.

Remington grinned again, then untied the two horses and handed the reins to Drew. With scarcely another word, he mounted his horse, picked up the mule's lead, and turned down the trail, headed north.

After Remington left, Drew went straight to the stream and scrubbed his hands. The water, bubbling and rushing along, now that the spring thaw had begun, numbed his fingers. Kate came up behind him.

"How long before we'll be leaving, Drew?"

"Huh? Oh, another couple of days, I reckon. Now that we have the horses, I suppose we could leave sooner, but I . . ." What excuse did he have, really? None. "I want to leave the

cabin hospitable for the next people who need it." That sounded good.

"Oh. Of course. I'll start cleaning this afternoon."

Kate felt the panic rise. Leaving the cabin. A couple of days. Now that they had the horses, they could be in Silverton in less than a week. Carson. He'd still be there. She couldn't let Drew walk into a trap, and that's exactly what it would be. A deadly trap, set to spring the minute Carson saw Drew alive and well. Tears stung her eyes. Fear gripped her heart. They couldn't go on to Silverton. What could she do? What could she say? The thought of her father raised no more emotion in her than seeing Remington ride off down the trail. Somehow, she had to keep Drew out of Silverton and away from Carson.

That night, after supper, Kate decided it was time to convince Drew to take her back to Laramie. Could she do it? He'd be angry. Maybe too angry to reason with. But if she could convince him, she'd keep him alive. That was worth enduring his wrath.

When they settled down in front of the fire, Drew pulled her close and kissed her. "Mighty good supper, Miss Mathison."

"Thank you kindly, Mr. Kingman."

The use of surnames had become a ritual between them now. A lot of things had become ritual. Kate took a deep breath.

"Drew?"

"Hmm?" He nuzzled her neck and reached for the buttons on her dress.

"I need to talk to you about something."

"Later." He unbuttoned another button, noticing that the dress seemed tighter on her lately. She'd put on some weight since they'd gotten here, and even the new dress she'd made was tight across her breasts.

"No, now." She pushed him away gently, then kissed him to make it all right.

Drew gave up and leaned back. "All right, woman, what is it now?"

"Now? What sort of a thing is that to say?" She stuck out her bottom lip, pouting.

Drew kissed the lip back into place. "I'm sorry. What is it?" He leaned back again and pulled her down on top of him.

Kate sighed. He could be so trying at times, but she still loved him. "I've . . . changed my mind about something."

"So? What's so unusual about that?" He caught her before she could sit up straight and silenced her with a kiss which almost cleared her mind of thought altogether.

Kate squirmed and sat up. "Will you listen, please? For once?" She knew that wasn't fair. Drew always listened to her, but he was being contrary and he needed to know it.

Drew bobbed his head up and down twice. "Yes, ma'am. I'm all ears." When Kate got into one of these moods, he'd learned to go along with it. Her dimples deepened when she felt put upon, and it was all he could do not to kiss them while she fussed at him.

"I've decided . . . I want to go back to Laramie." She said it fast, to get it out before she could back out. Then she waited for his reaction.

Drew fell completely silent for about half a minute. "Laramie? You want to go back to Laramie?"

She looked away, unable to meet his gaze straight on. "That's right. My father has taken care of himself for better than twenty years. There's no reason why he can't continue to do so." Flimsy. Would he believe it?

Drew propped himself up on one elbow. "Kate, that makes no sense whatsoever, and you know it."

"Why, of course it makes sense. It makes perfect sense." She got up from the floor and straightened her skirts, smoothed her hair, and patted her flaming cheeks. "Because we were forced to stay the winter here, I'm sure my father has either overpowered the claim jumpers who threatened his claim, or he's been killed by them or forced onto another claim. At any rate, it's none of my concern any longer, and I see no reason why we should journey on to Silverton when I shall surely be forced to leave immediately in order . . . in order to . . ." The wind went completely out of her sails. Drew had gotten up from the floor and turned her around. She hadn't looked at him yet. She didn't dare. The lies would be written all over her face.

"Kate, why don't you stop all this moralizing and tell me, straight out, what's stuck in your craw?"

She pulled away and rubbed the places on her arms where his hands had been. "Nothing is stuck in my craw, as you so indelicately put it. I've just made up my mind, that's all." Her throat started closing up. Her palms needed wiping on her skirts, yet her throat was as dry as dust. He turned her around again. The lack of anger in him was so totally unexpected, she hardly knew what to do next.

Drew tipped her chin upward with his fingers. "Kate?"

She looked at him briefly, then away. "What?"

"Tell me what's wrong." He waited. Then kissed her.

That did it. The walls tumbled and tears gushed along with the words swelling in her throat.

"We can't go to Silverton! You'll be killed if we go there!" She buried her face in his shirt and clamored to hold him closer.

"Killed? What in tarnation—?"

"Carson is there! When he sees you, he'll kill you where you stand! Don't you understand? We can't go to Silverton! Not while he's still there!" She looked at him finally, pleading with her eyes for him to hear and believe.

Drew's forehead, creased with confusion, smoothed. His mouth tightened into a straight line. "How do you know Carson is in Silverton?"

Kate swallowed hard. She'd have to tell him everything. That's when the anger would come. She'd deserve every bit of it.

"Carson was here."

"What? What nonsense is that? Carson quit following us before we ever got to this cabin."

Kate shook her head. "You were sick. The medicines I used weren't working. You were . . . you were . . . dying." She squeezed her eyes tightly shut and tried to stop the tears. "Carson and his men got here. He was going to kill you. I stopped him."

Drew couldn't believe what he was hearing. "You? Stopped him from killing me? How?"

The words were bitter. "I convinced him you were going to die anyway and that shooting a dying man would be a cowardly thing to do."

Drew nodded. "Carson is a decent man. I can see—"

"Decent! The man's vermin! If I could've killed him myself, I would have!"

The idea gave Drew an unexpected rush of pleasure. "You'd have killed him? To save me?"

"I'd've done anything to save you."

"Even then?"

Kate closed her eyes and buried her face in his chest again. "Even then."

"So, why didn't you?"

"I couldn't have killed them all, could I?"

"How many did he have with him?"

"Three white men."

Drew looked over the top of Kate's head. So. Carson had come and gone, leaving him for dead. That meant—"Wait a minute. Carson left me for dead. I can't believe he would've left you behind, too."

"He offered to take me to Silverton. I told him I'd rather die than go anywhere with him."

Drew smiled. He pictured it. Fire flashing in those smoky blue eyes. Spine straight as an aspen sapling. Yes, he could imagine the scene right well. The realization followed. Carson thought he was dead.

"Wait a minute, Kate. If I was as close to dead as you say, then how did I pull through?"

Kate smiled, remembering. "There was an Indian with Carson, too, and he gave me some herbs that night after the others were asleep. Told me to put them on the wound and make a tea from them, too. You got better so fast, I held my breath worrying that you would recover before Carson left and he'd kill you after all."

"What sort of herbs did he give you?"

"I don't know for sure, but I'm guessing comfrey and shepherd's purse and something else I didn't recognize. I didn't care. They saved your life, and that's all that mattered to me." She slipped her arms around his middle and hugged him close. "Please, Drew, let's go back to Laramie."

Drew thought it over. Running. He'd be running from Carson. Sooner or later, Carson would find him, or hear about him, and he'd have it all to do again. No. There'd be no more running.

"We're going to Silverton, Kate."

"No! We can't! Oh, please, Drew. Anything but that. I don't care about my father or his claim. He never cared a whit about us. Why should you risk your life for his sake? I only care about you. Just you. Please."

Drew wiped the tears from her cheeks and kissed her lips tenderly. "What a woman you are, Kate. If I searched the world over, I'd never find another one like you."

Kate said nothing. She knew he'd already made up his mind. They'd be going to Silverton and there was nothing she could do to change it.

"What are we going to do?"

"You leave things to me, Kate. I'll take care of us, now."

Chapter Twenty-Two

A sob caught in Kate's throat when she closed the cabin door for the last time. She'd known more happiness here than anywhere else on earth. If only they could stay right here, together, with no worries other than what to cook for supper, bringing more water from the creek, and waiting until the sun went down so they could love each other again.

A twinge in her belly stopped her for a moment. The baby had started to move only yesterday. She'd had a hard time keeping her pregnancy from Drew. When they'd made love last night—probably for the last time—he'd commented on how she'd gained weight since they'd gotten to the cabin. She'd laughed and told him she hadn't gotten enough exercise. It seemed to placate him for the time being. If he knew she was carrying his child, things could get complicated in a hurry.

The baby kicked again, prompting a smile from its mother. "Just you wait, little one," she whispered happily. "Your time will come."

If God had to be cruel and take Drew away from her, at least He'd seen fit to leave her with this child as a reminder of the love she'd shared in this mountain home.

Strange, how she'd come to think of it as home, but she knew why. It wasn't the cabin that felt like home. Being with Drew made it home.

"Ready, Kate?" Drew brought one of the horses over and offered to help her into the saddle.

Kate accepted the help gratefully. Already, she could tell a difference in her body from the added weight. Drew grunted a bit when he pushed her up into the saddle.

"You really have gained weight, woman."

"Hush, Drew. It isn't polite to speak of such things to a lady."

Drew grinned. "Yes, ma'am. Begging your pardon, ma'am."

A pain shot through her heart. Only days left. How could she bear it?

Drew checked the packs again. "Without the mule, we're having to leave a lot behind."

"For the next travelers in need of shelter," she mused, thinking how grateful she'd been to find all the things here last year that had made their stay comfortable.

"Time to go." Drew stepped up onto his horse and pulled up beside Kate. "Are you ready, Miss Mathison?"

"Quite ready, Mr. Kingman." She leaned toward him slightly and found him thinking identical thoughts.

His lips on hers felt warm and alive. His hand cradling her face made her limp with desire. His eyes trained on hers shone with—dare she let herself think it?—love. She had to tell him. Before they parted. He had to know how precious he'd become to her, even if it drove him away.

After much begging and pleading, Drew had agreed that she'd ride into Silverton alone and he would head south, away from Carson. To tell the truth, though, Drew had no intention of running away from Carson again, but he knew better than telling Kate. Let her think he was heading south, away from the danger. Let her get on with her life without him as soon as possible.

Damn. If Carson weren't in the picture, he'd beg Kate to come with him to Texas. But until he'd dealt with Carson one way or another, he had no business making promises for the future. Kate would be better off without him to worry about. If her father turned out to be the scoundrel Drew suspected, she'd more than have her hands full just tending to the old coot.

He wanted to tell her how he felt about her. His life had started to mean something when he met her on that dusty hill in Wyoming. But he couldn't do that. He couldn't say, "I love you, Kate," then "Good-bye." Damn. Seemed like his luck ought to change pretty soon. Up until now, it had been pretty poor, except for the months they'd spent together in this cabin.

They rode all day, saying little. Kate seemed lost in thought, too, and neither had felt the need for idle conversation.

They spent the night huddled beneath the blankets, just as they had before they reached the cabin. Drew wanted to make love to her again, but taking clothes off in this cold would be sheer foolishness. So he did the best in the situation and kissed her until they were both making those damned little noises he loved so much.

Kate couldn't get close enough to Drew. If only the weather would warm up enough for them to shed some of their clothes . . .

Drew kissed every inch of exposed skin he could find. A pain, deep inside, finally made him stop. He buried his face in her hair. "Kate, I'm so sorry."

"Sorry?" Had she heard him right? "There's nothing to be sorry for, Drew."

"There's everything to be sorry for. If I'd've gotten you to Silverton last year, if that damned bear hadn't gotten the best of me, if I hadn't killed Tom Carson—"

"Shhhh. It's all past us now, Drew. And I wouldn't change a single thing that's happened, even if I could. Except for you being hurt and so terribly sick. I'd change that."

But then he'd be dead from Carson's gun, Drew thought. Everything that had happened had worked together for good. Everything, that is, but the fact that he'd fallen in love with this woman when he had no business falling in love with anybody.

Anger built inside Drew until he nearly exploded. When they got to Silverton tomorrow, he'd find Carson and kill him, as hard as that would be. He'd have to kill the galoots with him, too. Then he'd haul Kate out of Silverton so fast, her head would swim. He'd take her to Texas to his ranch and they'd build up the herd again. It'd take years, but that wouldn't matter. They'd be together, holding each other every night the way they held each other now, only without all these damned clothes in the way. He squeezed her harder and harder.

"Drew, I can't breathe!" she whispered, and he loosened his grip.

"Sorry. I was just thinking."

"Thinking what?" Say it! Just once, she had to hear the words!

"Nothing. I guess we ought to get some shut-eye. We have a long ride tomorrow if we're to get to Silverton before dark."

"You really think we'll get there tomorrow?" No! They needed one more night together. Please, God, give them one more night.

"I 'spect so. Are you warm enough?"

"With your arms around me, I am." She snuggled closer to him, loving the way his breath warmed her face. Thinking back to the beginning of their trip, she smiled.

Drew felt the movement against his chin. "What are you thinking, woman?"

"Oh, I was just remembering the first night we slept close like this."

Drew laughed. "I was scared to death to touch you."

"And I was scared you wouldn't."

"Really? You wanted me to touch you?"

She'd given away too much. "Well, not exactly. It's just that I'd never . . . well, I was . . . oh, never mind."

Drew understood. She'd never been touched before. He was the only one who'd ever taken any liberties with her. Just look where that first night had led. This time, he was the one to smile.

"What, Drew?" She raised up just a bit, but he pushed her back down until she was nestled against him again.

"I was just thinking about that night on the ridge when I fell asleep thinking about Lucy, and woke up realizing I'd overstepped my boundaries with you."

"I remember. I was scared to wake you, scared not to. But it felt so good, I couldn't make you stop."

Drew took a long, deep breath. "When I woke up, Kate, and knew what I'd done, I want you to know that I stopped thinking about Lucy."

Kate trembled. "You were thinking about me?"

"Yep. No one else."

It was almost as good as having him say he loved her. "Drew, tell me about Lucy."

"I thought I did already."

"You did, but not a lot. Did you . . . did you love her?"

Drew thought about it for a minute. "I suppose, in a way, I did. We weren't married that long."

"But you asked her to marry you. That had to mean—"

"She'd lost her husband. I needed someone to care for my place. We got married because it was the sensible thing for both of us."

A wave of warmth rushed through Kate. "I see."

"When she died, I missed her something awful, but I don't suppose it'll be the same as I'll be feeling when . . ." Should he tell her? He wanted to tell her. More than anything.

"When . . . ?" she helped him, holding her breath.

"Well, that is, I think I'll miss you even more, Kate. We've shared more—That is, we've been through more together than I ever went through with Lucy." Awkward. Not at all what he wanted to say. What he needed to say.

203

"You mean with the bear and all?" Her voice was barely more than a whisper now.

"Yeah. But more than that. We've done a lot more . . . loving . . . than I ever did with Lucy." Damn, but they were talking about sensitive matters. And yet, it seemed right to be entirely honest with Kate. She'd saved his life. She'd saved his heart from dying of loneliness.

"I see." Kate wound one hand up around Drew's neck and twirled his hair in her fingers.

Drew shivered, but not from the cold. "Kate . . . ?"

"Yes, Drew?"

"I guess what I'm trying to say is . . ."

"Yes?"

He swallowed hard. He had to get them to Silverton tomorrow. If they spent one more night like this, in each other's arms, he'd end up telling her how he felt about her, and it wasn't right or good to hurt her like that. "Let's get some sleep. We have a long ride ahead of us tomorrow."

Kate squeezed her eyes shut.

CHAPTER TWENTY-THREE

Silverton at last.

Kate stood in the stirrups and brushed a wayward strand of hair off her face. In the dim light of dusk, the lights of Silverton reflected off the snow-capped peaks surrounding the mountain mining village.

"There it is, Kate." Drew let out a long sigh. "Any idea where your father's claim is?"

"None at all. I suppose I'll have to ask around in town until someone gives me directions to find him."

They'd hardly spoken for the past few hours. Finality surrounded them like the towering peaks. Kate hated the sight of the town she'd struggled so hard to reach.

Drew got down from his horse. "I can't leave you to ride in alone, Kate."

Kate looked at him sharply. "But that's what we agreed on, Drew. You can't go into Silverton. If Carson sees you—"

"Then he sees me. I can't run from him all my life." He reached for her and helped her to the ground. "Try to understand. The running I've already done is choking me. I have to settle things with him, one way or the other."

Kate understood, but she wasn't about to let him see that she did. "You're a stubborn mule, Drew Kingman."

"I am at that. But I promised to see you safely to your pa, and I'll be damned if I'll stop short now." He scratched his chin thoughtfully. "And, if your pa has struck silver like he said, I'll be wanting to collect that reward you offered me in Laramie for escorting you from there to here."

"You rascal. If you think for a minute I believe you did this for the money—"

"Why, of course I did it for the money. I'll need a passel of money to rebuild my herd once I get back to Texas." If he ever got back to Texas. He ran his fingers through her hair. She closed her eyes and leaned toward him. He kissed her lightly, and pulled her against him.

"Will I ever see you again, Drew?"

"Someday, maybe. It'll take a lot of work to get that ranch going again." If he lived long enough. He knew she was thinking the same thoughts. "We'd best get into town before it gets any darker. There's supposed to be a fancy new hotel here where we can find a room for the night."

"Two rooms," she said softly.

He nodded. Damn. Two rooms.

"Drew, I want to thank you again for all you've done to get me here." Her heart was breaking as surely as if Jerome Carson's hands were crushing the life out of her. "I'm much obliged to you for taking such good care of me."

"I wish things could be different."

"I know. Let's just leave it."

Drew nodded and kissed the top of her head before he kissed her mouth. It could be the last time. Damn. The last time!

They got on their horses and rode into Silverton.

There was little going on out in the snow-packed streets. Twangy chords of a player piano came from several establishments along Blair Street.

Drew steered them away from the merriment and they headed for the Grand Hotel.

"What's going on over there?" She pointed to a decrepit building where a man was being thrown out into the street.

"You don't want to know."

"A saloon? You forget, I was raised in a saloon."

"You weren't raised in a saloon like the ones in Silverton. Their main business isn't liquor sales, if you catch my meaning."

She did. Her face colored appropriately. "But there are so many of them. Are you sure—"

"I'm sure. Come on and let's get to the hotel."

The building looked to be brand new, with its mansard roof and a battery of dormer windows. Inside the lobby, there was a restaurant and a massive mahogany bar with fine mirrors. The place was packed with miners, gamblers, and traveling men, most of them too drunk to stand or walk straight. Kate stuck close to Drew while he arranged for two rooms, side by side, on the second floor.

"Come on. We'll get something to eat after we wash up."

Kate nodded and followed him up the stairs, wide-eyed and eager to see everything. She searched every face, wondering if she'd recognize her father if she saw him. Seeing no one at all familiar, she gave up the quest.

Drew unlocked the door to her room and set her bundle inside. "I'll be next door if you need me, Kate."

"Couldn't you come in now?"

A gentleman with a lady on his arm came out of a room three doors down and escorted her to the stairs. He tipped his hat to Drew when they passed.

"I think we'd best put on our best behavior, Miss Mathison. After all, I was hired to escort you to Silverton. It would seem improper if I were to be seen leaving your room." The pain in his voice came from his heart.

"I see. You're right, as usual, Mr. Kingman." Kate nodded politely, hoping she wouldn't cry in front of him, and went into the room, closing the door behind her.

Drew stood there in the hall for a moment, thinking how absurd this charade was getting to be, then he went into the room next door and straight to the wash basin on the chiffonier. He poured water from a pitcher into a bowl, washed his face and hands, then dried them on a towel lying beside the bowl. This was a fancy hotel, all right. He'd heard about it being built last year, but never had the opportunity to visit Silverton to see for himself if it really was the finest hotel on the western slope, as the builders claimed. Right now, though, with Kate next door—she might as well have been a thousand miles away—it didn't make a lot of difference to him. He figured he'd better change clothes before supper.

Kate washed carefully in the cold water and changed to a clean dress. She'd been able to sew two new dresses from the supplies in the sewing chest, and it felt good to put on something clean after their long ride.

The room was furnished quite nicely, with a four-poster bed sporting a generous feather mattress and hand-sewn quilts of rose and moss-green materials. Lace curtains framed the windows, and portraits of grim-looking men and women hung on the flowered wallpaper. Kate thought of the Prancing Horse in Laramie and Meg McGruder, and a smile crossed her lips. If only Meg could be here.

The baby kicked again. It had been especially active since mid-afternoon, and Kate had had a difficult time keeping such rambunctious behavior from Drew.

Was there a doctor in Silverton? How could she find out without arousing suspicion? How could she admit to anyone she was pregnant without benefit of wedlock? She'd be shunned by everyone, and the child would suffer most of all.

Kate gritted her teeth. Her child wasn't going to grow up ashamed.

An idea came to her then, and once she'd considered it, she

decided it would do nicely. Of course, she'd have to wait until Drew left Silverton for it to work, but since she expected him to be leaving tomorrow, it shouldn't pose a problem. If only she could find Pa. A knock at the door startled her. It was Drew, looking spiffy in a clean shirt, a paper collar, and nankeen trousers. She recognized them—the same trousers he'd worn when he'd taken her to supper in Laramie. He'd shaved, too, and combed his hair. He straightened his coat and shined the toes of his boots on the back of his britches.

"You look nice, Drew."

"So do you, Kate. Let's get something to eat. I'm near starved."

"Me, too."

They went downstairs to the restaurant. The man standing near the door led them to a table close to the front windows. Kate tried not to look directly into Drew's eyes, fearing her love for him would be apparent to everyone in the restaurant. It was powerful important for her to make the right impression in Silverton if the people here were to accept her as a proper lady.

Drew tugged at his paper collar and Kate laughed out loud.

"What's so funny?" Drew seemed self-conscious as all get-out in his fancy duds.

"You did that in Laramie." She put her hand in front of her mouth to stifle her giggles.

"Did what in Laramie?"

"Pulled at your collar. I wondered if I should suggest that you loosen the collar, but decided it wouldn't be proper."

"Oh, you did, did you?"

"Yes, I did. Would you like to loosen your collar, Mr. Kingman?"

"If I do, my head will fall off, Miss Mathison."

This brought a new burst of giggles from Kate. She was still laughing when a woman came to their table to take their order for supper.

"Have you decided what you'd like to eat?" the woman asked.

Kate swung around and stared at her. She knew that voice! "May Belle?"

The waitress stared. "Kate?" She looked around quickly to see if anyone had heard. "Shhhh. Here, I'm May Pearl."

Kate lowered her voice. "May Pearl? But why?"

Drew cleared his throat. "Excuse me, but do you two know each other?"

"Know each other?" Kate's eyes were as round as snowballs. "This is the . . . woman . . . who raised me."

Drew took a quick look at May Belle or May Pearl, whatever her name was. "The whore?" he whispered.

"Watch it, buster. In this fancy joint, I'm a waitress."

"Oh. Sorry." Drew flashed Kate a crooked smile and covered his eyes with one hand.

"What are you doing here?" Kate whispered. "You didn't say anything about leaving Sutterfield when I saw you last."

"It came up kind of sudden-like. We'll have time to talk later. I have to take your order now. The boss is giving me the evil eye."

Kate and Drew looked at the menu and ordered quickly. May Belle gave Kate a smile and Drew a smirk and left to turn in their orders to the kitchen.

"Well, at least you'll have one friend in Silverton," Drew said, holding back a grin.

"She was like a second mother to me, Drew. May Belle couldn't help what she was. She was always good to me and Ben."

"I know." Drew laid his hand on the table, palm up. "I'm sorry."

Kate placed her hand in his, suddenly unconcerned about

what it might look like. "It's all right." She knew Drew understood.

When May Belle brought their plates, piled high with steaks and boiled potatoes with spiced crab apples on the side, she leaned down to whisper into Kate's ear.

"I'm on the top floor, second door on the left. Come up later. I get off at ten."

"Thanks. I'll try."

"If you don't make it tonight . . ." She eyed Drew appraisingly. ". . . then I'll see you in the morning."

Kate noticed the look and blushed to match the red tablecloth. "In the morning, then."

May Belle leaned down again. "He sure is a looker, honey. I'm gonna wanta know how you met up with him."

"It's a long story."

"I'm wondering, too, where Ben's got off to."

Tears stung Kate's eyes. "It's a sad story."

May Belle seemed to get the drift. "Later." She stood up, cleared her throat, and boomed, "If y'all need anything else, just let me know."

Kate matched her volume. "We shall, May Pearl. Thank you kindly."

May Belle disappeared into the wad of customers.

Drew grinned like an ape.

Kate avoided his eyes, feeling embarrassed for some reason, and fiddled with a strand of hair that refused to lie straight. "What are you grinning about, Mr. Kingman?"

Drew laid his hand on the table again. "Nothing at all, Miss Mathison. Meeting your mama was a pleasure. A real pleasure."

"She's not my mama." Kate felt badly to feel ashamed of May Belle. "But she sure as shootin' took care of us when we needed somebody."

Drew turned his hand over, palm up again. "I know, Kate.

It's all right."

Kate studied his eyes for a minute to see if he was still funning her or if he was serious. She decided it was the latter and laid her hand in his. "Thanks, Drew."

"Any time, dear lady."

Kate wanted to get up from the table and wrap her arms around Drew and kiss him right here in front of everyone. In fact, if she couldn't kiss him soon, she thought she might die. Who cared what anyone thought? This might be her last chance . . .

"Mr. Kingman?"

"Yes, Miss Mathison?"

"I have a request of you."

"Name it, Miss Mathison."

"Take me upstairs and make love to me until I can't breathe without gasping, please."

Drew's smile disappeared. Blatant desire replaced it. "Anything you say, Miss Mathison."

Chapter Twenty-Four

Kate woke up slowly the next morning, stretched, reached for Drew, then remembered he'd left quietly before dawn. Still protecting her reputation. Bless his heart.

A knock brought a smile. "Yes?"

"Kate? It's May Belle. Let me in."

"May Belle?" Kate jumped from the bed, wiggled into her clothes, and opened the door. "I'm sorry I . . . well, I didn't make it last night."

"That's all right, honey. Can I come in?"

"Of course!" Kate stepped back and closed the door behind her. "It's so good to see you again!" She hugged the aging woman and debated whether or not she should tell her the truth, half the truth, or manufacture a lie.

"You're pregnant, aren't you?" May Belle's eyes bored through her.

"How did you know?" Kate turned away to hide her embarrassment. "That is, whatever do you mean? Of course I'm not . . . pregnant."

May Belle pulled her around and smiled the smile of a woman about to become a grandmother. "Now, child, there's no need trying to hide the truth from me. I know you too well. And I'm a woman."

Kate gave up any pretense and collapsed in May Belle's arms. "Oh, May Belle, I've made such a mess of my life."

They sat down on the edge of the bed. Kate leaned against

her dear friend and blubbered.

"Now, now, child. Tell old May Belle everything."

"Everything?" Kate felt like a little girl again.

"Start with when you left Sutterfield."

Kate sat up, blew her nose on a hanky, and told the story from beginning to end. Or until the present time, which, she confessed to May Belle, wasn't nearly the end.

"And I love him!" Kate blubbered some more. "What on earth am I going to do? I can't just let him ride off to Texas, but I can't let him stay here any longer for fear he'll get killed. I wish I knew what to do."

May Belle patted her back and stroked her hair, just as she'd done a thousand times while Kate was growing up. "Well, honey, it's a puzzler, that it is. But there's a solution. Go with Drew to Texas."

Kate sat up. "He hasn't asked me, May Belle. I can't just announce that I'm going with him, can I?"

"He hasn't asked you because he loves you too much to raise your hopes of a future together as long as this sidewinder, Carson, is on his trail. If he'd asked you to go with him, I wouldn't have given two cents for him. From what you've told me, he's a decent man, and easy on the eyes to boot."

Easy on the eyes was an understatement, and they both knew it. Kate stopped crying and tried to be tougher. "What if I tell Drew I want to go with him to Texas and he tells me no? What then?"

"I don't know, honey bunch. But I think you ought to tell him how you feel about him. Lands sakes, it isn't often a woman finds a man to love the way you love Drew. And with the young 'un to think about, you don't have much choice. You're gonna have to fight for your man—and your child. Without a name, it'll be more than either of you can bear. Believe me, I know."

Kate straightened her spine. "I've already decided what to do about that problem, May Belle. After all, Ben was killed on this trip. As far as anyone knows, he was my husband. My child will have the name Mathison."

"But what about Caleb?"

Kate thought about him for the first time. "He's here?"

"Sure as shooting. Once people know you're his daughter—"

"Daughter-in-law, May Belle. Pa will go along with it, or I'll wring his scrawny neck." Kate stuck out her chin defiantly.

May Belle smiled and shook her head. "I reckon he will, honey. My, but you have his spunk." She smiled proudly. "By the way, he's anything but scrawny. Caleb hasn't missed many meals since he came to Silverton five years ago."

"Well, I'll wring his fat neck, then. Do you know where I can find him?"

"Yep. In fact, I'll send word to him that you're here, but not to tell a soul until he sees you. You can explain everything to him—and if you need some help, I'll straighten him out good and proper."

"What would I do without you?" Kate hugged her neck and swallowed the last of the tears. A knock prompted them to stand, straighten skirts and waists, and dab at their noses before opening the door.

"Drew. I'm so glad to see you." Kate ushered him inside in a hurry. "I have something to tell you. I've—"

"Changed your mind again. I figured as much. What is it this time?" He turned to May Belle. "Good morning, ma'am. I'm sorry if I seemed a bit too abrupt last night."

"Think nothing of it, Mr. Kingman. In fact, I wish to thank you."

"For what?"

"For seeing Kate here to Silverton safe and sound. I'll be beholden to you for the rest of my life. If there's ever anything I can do for you—"

Kate elbowed her.

"Uh, that is, if I may be of service to you—"

"May Belle!"

"Lands sakes, child! He knows what I'm talking about!"

Drew laughed. "I do indeed, ma'am, and I appreciate the offer."

"Well, I'll be getting on downstairs. I have to go to work in a few hours and I have a few chores to take care of first." She winked at Kate. "I'll be seeing both of you later." May Belle gave Kate a kiss on the cheek and patted her hand affectionately. "Remember what I told you, honey. Anything worth having is worth fighting for."

"I'll remember." Kate felt the tightness in her throat. Since she'd been with child, tears came easy. But, she was determined not to cry during the next speech she had to make.

After May Belle excused herself, Drew immediately held out his arms to Kate and she came to him eagerly.

"I missed you." He kissed her tenderly and rubbed her back the way he usually did after they'd made love.

"You've been away only a few hours."

"They were long hours."

"Drew, I have something to tell you."

"Let me guess. Your pa is really in California. Or Nevada. Or is it Boston?" A smile broke through in spite of his efforts to stay solemn.

"Don't tease me, Drew. What I have to tell you is deadly serious." Could she actually say the words to him? What would he do? Leave without saying good-bye? Tell her she was crazy and walk out of her life forever?

"All right, Kate. Can I kiss you first, though?"

How could she say no? Instead of words she used her body to tell him the answer. Drew groaned and held her against him while he loved her mouth, her neck, her eyelids, and then her mouth again.

"Stop, Drew. If we don't stop—"

"I have to go, Kate."

The words were like icy water poured over her head. "Leave? But you can't leave yet! I haven't found Pa and—"

"May Belle can help you find him, and you know it." He looked straight into her eyes. "God, but you're beautiful." Kate stiffened in his arms. "He's here, isn't he? Carson. You've seen him."

Drew nodded. "I've sent word to him that we're going to settle things between us, once and for all."

"Drew, no! You can't! He'll kill you before you have a chance—"

"There's not to be any explaining, Kate. The time for explaining has passed. I can't live my life running from Carson or any man."

"But, Drew—"

He covered her mouth with two fingers, then kissed her lips softly. "No more, Kate. It's done. I came to say good-bye."

"But I was going to tell you—"

"Save it. If I'm able to listen once this is over, I'll hear you out. If not, then . . ." He owed it to her. She deserved to hear the words. "I love you, Kate."

"Love me? You love me?" Her heart swelled until she thought it would burst.

"I have for a long time. If I'm still breathing after I see Carson, I'll have something to talk to you about, too."

Kate threw her arms around his neck. "Don't go, Drew! We'll go to Texas! We'll go back east! Anywhere, away from Carson and—"

"You haven't been listening, Kate. It's done."

"You just can't say you love me and then walk in front of Carson's guns. I love you too much to let you do it." She clung

217

to him fiercely, felt his hands running up and down her spine, wished with all her heart and soul she could magically take them away from this horrid town!

Drew buried his face in her hair. "I suspected you might be loving me, too. It's nice to know."

"Of course I love you. I adore you! My life is nothing without you. Please, Drew, please—"

"No more, Kate. I have to go now. Carson is waiting. This is something I have to do. Otherwise, I wouldn't be much of a man for you to love."

Kate knew he was right. Self-respect meant everything to a man like him. "All right. If you've set your mind on it, I guess there's nothing I can say or do to change it."

Drew kissed her once more, then turned and left before she could say another word.

Her heart, her whole world lay shattered at her feet. It wasn't fair. Life just wasn't fair. The baby! She didn't tell him about the baby! Surely, that would change his mind. Kate ran to the door and jerked it open. She almost ran into a man standing in the hall.

"Excuse me. I'm sorry. I have to go. I—"

"Katy?"

Kate stopped and stared at the man. "Pa?"

"Well, if it's not my little Katy-bug, you can dip me in the creek and call me Shorty! Come 'ere, young 'un and give your old pa a hug." The barrel-chested man grabbed Kate and swung her around.

His beard scratched her cheek, but she hardly noticed. Pa! Alive and well and—"Pa!"

"That's me, darlin'. Let's go downstairs and have some breakfast. We've got a lot of catching up to do. Where's Ben?" He looked inside her room.

"Ben . . . Ben's dead, pa. He fell off his horse about two days out of Sutterfield and—"

"Oh, now that's real poor news, Katy darlin'. How on earth did you get here without Ben?"

"I can't explain now, Pa. We have to hurry. Please!" She grabbed his arm and hauled him down the stairs as fast as her skirts would allow.

"Whoa, there, Katy. I'm an old man now. I can't be taking the stairs at a gallop this way." He lagged behind just enough to slow her pace.

"But he's leaving, Pa. We have to stop him. He doesn't know—"

"Doesn't know what? That you're trying to make an old codger like me move faster than he's moved in ten years? Who's leaving?"

Kate left him halfway down the last flight of stairs and ran to the front door. She pushed her way through a crowd of miners coming in and frantically searched the street. There wasn't a sign of Drew anywhere!

"No!" she screamed. "Drew! Come back!"

Caleb Mathison caught up to his daughter and finally persuaded her to come inside with him. Deflated, Kate went with him to a table in the restaurant and sat down, peering out the front windows, hoping for any sign of Drew.

"Want some breakfast?" When she didn't answer, he ordered steak and eggs for both of them. "Why don't you tell me what's wrong, Katy?"

Katy. She hadn't been called Katy since she was five years old, since before he'd left the family and run off with some foolish dream of discovering gold or silver or rubies or whatever the miners happened to think they could find in these infernal Rocky Mountains. The anger boiled up inside her and spilled out.

"You want to know what's wrong?" She straightened in the

chair. "You're what's wrong, that's what."

"Me? But you got my telegram and now you're here. What's wrong with that?"

"The man I love is going to be killed because I'm here."

"Whoa, darlin', you're gonna have to start a little farther back. What you're sayin' makes no sense at all. Who is this man?"

"Drew Kingman. After Ben was killed, I hired him to bring me here. We would've been here last October, but he was almost killed by a bear and we had to spend the winter in the mountains."

"Wait a minute. You spent the winter on the mountain?"

"There was a cabin there. A skinner stole our horses, but he brought them back. We weren't able to travel until the thaw."

Caleb shook his head, as though he had something loose in there that needed stirring. "I'm not following you very well, Katy."

"Stop calling me that! You haven't cared anything about me for better than twenty years. Mama died of a broken heart, way before she died in the fire when our house burned."

"I heard about that. I'm real sorry. I loved your mama."

"Well, you sure picked a strange way to show it. Why didn't you come for us after she died? Why did you leave us to be raised by strangers?"

Caleb shook his head and looked down at the table. "I couldn't. I hardly had bread to eat myself. And, where I was living was no place for young 'uns. You were better off in Sutterfield."

"Better off living in the back of a saloon? Better off being treated like dirt? Better off alone in the world?" Kate wanted to scream her fury, but she thought better of it in such a public place. Anyway, it would do no good after twenty years of storing up the heartbreak and anger. It was plain to see he hadn't changed a whit since the last time she'd seen him.

"What can I say, except I'm dreadful sorry? Considering all you've just said, I'm finding it hard to believe you and Ben were coming in answer to my telegram."

Kate leaned toward him across the table and dropped her voice to a mere whisper. "I'll tell you why we were coming. We were coming for our share of the silver. For a chance to live comfortably for once in our lives, without having to scrape and scratch for every meal we had. We came for the silver."

Caleb bowed his head.

Kate knew. "There's no silver, is there?"

Caleb looked at her squarely for a minute before he spoke. "Not yet. But we're close. Before too much longer, we're gonna hit that mother lode and—"

"Drew was right. You were afraid of claim jumpers and you lied to get us here to help you keep your name on a worthless hole in the ground." She would've cried if it would've helped, but there didn't seem to be any use in it. "And now, Drew is going to die."

"You haven't explained that part yet, Katy. Sorry. What do you want me to call you?"

All the fight had gone out of her. "Katy is fine, Pa. It doesn't matter any more. Nothing matters any more."

"But it does, Katy darlin'." His eyes sparkled with new interest. "All we have to do is keep after that mine and—"

"Haven't the jumpers taken it away from you by now?"

"Oh, yeah, they took it for a while, but I talked them into letting me back on the place last November."

"Talked them into it? Who are these claim jumpers that they'd let you talk them into giving the mine back?"

Caleb scratched his nose with the back of one hand. "Well, I guess that's something I haven't told you yet. I think it's best we wait until later. Tell me about this feller you're so all-fired worried about."

"Drew Kingman. I love him."

Caleb squinted at her. "Does he love you, too?"

"Told me so just today."

"Well, then?"

"There's a man tracking him. Jerome Carson. Do you know him?"

"Yep. Fine feller. Why's he so riled up at Kingman?"

"Drew killed his brother. He wants revenge."

"Can't blame him for that."

"His brother was a cattle thief. Drew tracked him down to get back the money from selling the stolen cattle and the sidewinder pulled a gun on him."

"Has Kingman told this to Carson?"

"Nope. Carson intends to kill Drew on sight. I told Carson myself about his no-good brother, but it didn't do a bit of good."

Caleb nodded and scratched his grizzled chin. "Well, now, there may still be time to do something before these two young fellers decide to kill each other. Are you sure you love this man, Katy?"

Kate leaned forward again. "I love him so much, I'm carrying his child, Pa."

Caleb's eyes lit up like lightning bugs. "Glory be! I'm gonna be a grandpa!"

"What can we do?"

Caleb looked around the restaurant until he spied May Belle, just coming in the front door. "May Belle. Over here."

"Caleb, I've told you a hundred times, it's May Pearl. Kate, we have to hurry."

"It's all right, May Belle . . . uh Pearl. Pa has a plan to save Drew."

"It better be quick. They're down the street. Carson just called him out."

CHAPTER TWENTY-FIVE

Drew got up from the chair he'd been sitting in for the past fifteen minutes in the Bull's Head Saloon.

"Come on out here, Kingman!" Carson yelled from the street. "There's no use in hurting innocent people."

"I'm coming!" Drew yelled back, and pushed the chair back under the table. Others in the saloon stopped their chatter. They stared at Drew with fear in their eyes. When he walked toward the door, they scattered—behind the bar, through the back doors, under tables, and into corners. Drew shook his head at them. They'd be safe because Carson had it in his mind to kill only one man today.

Drew stood in the door for a minute to get his bearings. Carson was standing in the middle of Blair Street. Three more men flanked him. A real fair fight. Four against one—perfect odds for someone wanting to blast a man into hell.

"Come out, Kingman!" Carson shouted again. "I won't let you shoot me in the back like you shot my brother."

A murmur of disapproval came from the cowering patrons of the Bull's Head.

Drew took two steps out on the porch. The doors swung behind him until they settled into their familiar niche in the doorframe.

"I didn't shoot your brother in the back, Jerome. My bullets went through him from front to back. If you'd've taken time to ask those who saw it happen, you'd know that."

223

"Not how I heard it."

Drew said nothing. His best friend wasn't interested in explanations.

"I mean to kill you." The look on Carson's face wasn't hatred—it reflected deep pain.

Drew nodded in resignation. "Tell your friends we don't need any help settling this."

Carson hesitated momentarily, then nodded to his men to leave them alone. "I don't need any help killing you, that's for sure. Come out in the street. I've come a lot of miles for this. I'm ready to put you in the ground."

After Carson's men had retreated to the sidewalks, Drew walked slowly to the center of the street. The crunch of snow beneath his feet was the only sound to be heard. Drew knew enough about Carson to believe that he wouldn't shoot him down without a fair draw. At least he hoped he wouldn't. In this day and age, there was no telling what one man might do when pushed far enough.

"First, I want the money you stole from Tom," Carson demanded.

"A man can't steal what belongs to him. Your brother got that money selling the beeves he stole from me. I took back what was mine—what was left of it, that is, after Tom spent half of it on liquor and women." Why hadn't he shot him already? Drew never would've believed it would go on this long. Maybe their friendship ran deeper than blood after all.

"You're not only a thief and a killer, you're a liar, too." Carson widened his stance. "Get ready to die."

"No!" Kate screamed the word from the time she reached the street until she planted herself squarely in front of Drew. "You'll not kill him, Jerome Carson! Not now, or ever! Your brother was scum, plain and simple. You can ask the people of this town if he wasn't!"

"Kate, get out of the street!" Drew shouted at her.

She whirled around to face him, being careful to stay exactly between the two men. "No, Drew. I won't let him kill you when his thieving brother deserved to die."

"Get out of the way, ma'am," Carson said in a deadly flat voice. "Getting a woman to plead your case only proves your guilt, Kingman. Get your whore out of the way or I'll kill her, too."

Kate bristled from head to toe. "You dare to call me a *whore?*" She stomped closer to Carson with a look on her face that should have turned him to stone where he stood. "You've tracked an innocent man halfway across this country without checking to see whether or not he might be telling the truth about your dear, departed, cattle-thieving brother. What does that make you, Mr. Carson? It makes you a fool. If you'd taken the opportunity to ask anyone who witnessed what happened between your brother and Drew Kingman, you never would've left Wyoming."

"She's right. Tom Carson was no good from the time he started to pack a gun."

May Belle stomped her way out to stand beside Kate, glaring at Jerome Carson with a look that could've melted his gun barrel.

"You came to visit me regularly enough in Sutterfield, or don't you remember? Your brother also got to be a regular visitor when he was in Montana. After his second 'visit' I threw him out!"

Carson squinted at the redheaded woman barreling toward him from the far side of the street. "May Belle? What in tarnation are you doing in Silverton?"

"Stopping you from killing a man you oughtn't to be a killing. You're a good man, unlike that scum of a brother of yours. Don't throw pride after foolishness. Don't kill this man until you know for sure exactly what happened."

Carson hesitated.

Drew didn't like the way things were going. Women, taking up for him!

"Enough!" Drew yelled loudly enough to startle everyone on the street, including Carson. "Let's get this over with. I didn't want to kill Tom, and I don't want to kill you, but that seems to be what you're wanting, so let's get it over with." Drew looked straight at Kate. "Get out of the street."

Kate swallowed hard. May Belle backed up and planted herself on the sidewalk with one hand over her heart. Carson looked from May Belle to Kate to Drew, then settled his stance.

Last chance. Only one thing left to try. Kate walked over to where Carson could hear her but Drew could not. She spoke so softly that Carson had to strain to catch the words.

"Mr. Carson, I think you're a decent man. May Belle tells me you are—and so does Drew. If you're still convinced beyond any doubt that Drew Kingman murdered your brother, then I guess you're going to have to do what your honor demands and kill him. But let me tell you this. If you kill him, be ready to kill me next, because I won't rest until I've put a bullet through your heart." Lifting her chin high, she turned and walked toward May Belle.

Drew watched her go. His eyes connected with hers one last time, then he faced Jerome Carson.

Jerome Carson, hands poised above the gun in its holster on his right hip, ran his tongue over dry lips.

A scream pierced the air, then stopped with a muffled cry.

Drew recognized that scream and forgot about Carson. Searching the crowd lined up on the sidewalk outside the saloon, his blood raced when he couldn't find Kate. May Belle came rushing out of the saloon, pointing back inside as she ran toward Drew.

"They took her! They're headed into the mountains!" She pointed the way.

Drew stared at Carson for a long moment. "Help me."

Carson nodded.

Kate couldn't see anything. Whoever had grabbed her had tied a bandanna around her eyes so she couldn't see where they were taking her. They'd also stuffed a rag into her mouth so she couldn't keep screaming. Terrified, Kate struggled against the knotted rope binding her wrists, but there was no use shredding her skin. There was no way to escape.

"Quit squirming. We aren't going to hurt you."

She wanted to believe it, but being kidnapped off a street in broad daylight didn't exactly add credibility to their words. She decided to wait until they arrived at wherever they were taking her. She'd save her strength and try to get away then.

Drew and Carson rode hard in the direction May Belle pointed, but the absence of tracks soon convinced them the kidnappers had backtracked to throw them off the trail once they were out of town.

Searching the ground carefully, Drew purposefully avoided conversation until Carson broke the silence.

"She's a fine woman. Where did you find her?"

"In the dirt outside Sutterfield. Her horse threw her just after her brother was killed. Snake spooked the horses."

"So you brought her along. Why?"

"Why not? She needed to find her pa. I couldn't leave a woman alone, without escort."

Carson nodded. "I get the feeling she's more than someone you're escorting to her pa."

Drew took a deep breath and looked at Carson—Jerome—his

friend—for the first time since they'd left town. "I love her, Jerome."

"I could tell." He looked away, released a huge sigh, then looked back. "How did we get so far from home?"

Drew knew what he meant. How had they gone from being close friends since childhood to pointing guns at each other with intent to kill?

"*We* didn't."

Jerome ducked his head, embarrassed to look Drew straight in the eye.

"I don't want to kill you. And I don't want you to kill me."

"Where does that leave us? You killed Tom. From what I heard, you shot him in the back."

"Who told you that?"

Jerome tilted his head back and closed his eyes. "Chester."

"Tom's sidekick. What makes you think he'd tell the truth? He was with Tom when they stole my herd."

Jerome looked straight into Drew's eyes. "Tell me the truth. I'll know if you lie."

Drew stood and smiled at his friend. "Tom and three others rounded up my herd about dawn and headed north with them. I found Tom's canteen after they were gone. By the time I found the herd, Tom had sold every last head and left for Montana. I went after my money. When I caught up to them, they were drunk out of their minds—passed out in the saloon. I pulled the money from their pockets. More than half of what they got for my herd was gone. I intended to leave them there, but Tom woke up and saw me. He pulled himself up from the floor, reaching for his gun. I aimed at his arm, but he lost his footing and fell. My bullet went through his chest. Front to back. I didn't want to kill him. God help me, I tried to get him to a doctor in time to stop the bleeding, but he was dead before I could get him out of the saloon."

Jerome nodded. "That sounds like the friend I had in Texas. I'm sorry, Drew, for putting you through all this. I couldn't believe you'd shoot Tom in cold blood. But that's what everyone said."

Drew held out his hand. Jerome took it and they shook in friendship for the first time in months.

"Now, let's find Kate. I'm obliged for your help."

"That's what friends are for. Let's find her."

CHAPTER TWENTY-SIX

Of all the sorry luck. Kate cursed the men who'd tied her to this saddle like a sack of potatoes. She couldn't see where they were going because they'd tied a dirty kerchief around her eyes. It smelled like sweat and made her want to puke. They'd also gagged her with another filthy kerchief after she refused to quit screaming for them to stop and let her go.

Only thing to do now was rest and gain some strength to fight them once they finally decided to let her down from this swaybacked horse. If she had the chance to get her fingernails anywhere close to their ugly faces, she'd—

The horse slowed, snorted, and lowered his head to graze. Kate tensed, waiting for one of them to come and get her out of the saddle. But they didn't. She heard footsteps and a door creaking open, then bumping closed.

Within a minute, though, the door bumped again and she heard them talking. The hammer of a gun clicked back before rough hands reached for her. So much for clawing his eyes out. She'd have to wait until one of them wasn't standing there with a gun aimed at her.

"I'm gonna take the gag outta your mouth now, Kate. Don't you bite me or I'll have to do something I don't wanna do."

Kate nodded. She'd agree to anything to get these smelly things off her face. How dare this scoundrel call her by her given name?

He untied the knots in the back, then pulled both kerchiefs

off at the same time. Kate coughed to be free of the gag and squinted. The sun shone over the man's left shoulder, blinding her. She couldn't see his face at all.

The other man took several steps toward her. "Damn. I never thought he wuz tellin' the truth, Sam. But he wuz, for sure. Lookit those eyes. And that hair. And lookit her nose. Hot damn. The old man told the truth for once in his sorry life."

Who were they talking about, and what was all the commotion about how she looked? What difference did it make? The only people she knew in this town were her father and May Belle. Could the "old man" be her father?

"Why did you bring me here?" she demanded. "I don't have any money or jewels or gold or anything of value."

"He'll listen to reason to get you back, Kate."

"My name is Kate Mathison. I would appreciate it if you'd call me Miss Mathison."

They hee-hawed with laughter at that, slapping their knees and snorting through their noses.

"What is so funny about my name?"

"She don't know!" They laughed some more.

The one called Sam took her arm. "Come on inside, Miss Mathison, and set a spell. I reckon there's thangs you need to know about your pa."

Kate felt a chill run down her spine. What were they talking about? If Drew were here—Oh, dear God. Drew! She'd completely forgotten about him—and Carson. What if Carson had killed him? Tears burned her eyes, but she refused to let these galoots see her cry. If Drew survived the fight, he'd be coming to look for her. If not, her father would find out she'd been kidnapped and follow. Either way, she'd have the pleasure of kicking these swine right where it would hurt the most.

She blushed with the thought, then banished her embarrassment. How dare they abduct a woman—a pregnant woman!—

and treat her so poorly? They'd pay for it. She'd see to it.

Drew motioned to Carson to ease forward alongside him.

"There." Drew pointed toward a cabin just below the ridge. "You go around that way. We'll try to surprise them."

Carson nodded and disappeared into the trees.

If they hurt her, Drew would kill them without a second thought. He spied Carson behind a tree on the edge of the clearing where the cabin sat and signaled him to stay put until both of them were in position.

Just as Drew reached the corner of the cabin, the door slammed open and Kate emerged, ranting about "that no-good, sorry varmint!"

Drew stepped out from the side of the cabin, his gun pointed toward the two men who'd followed Kate onto the porch, and thumbed back the hammer. "Hold it right there. Kate, come here."

"Drew! You're alive! She took one step toward him, then spied Carson approaching from the other side of the clearing. She reversed her course and headed straight for Carson with her hands raised, fingers curved into claws. "Don't shoot him, you bastard! I'll gouge your eyes out before I'll let you hurt him!"

Carson caught her by the wrists and held her away from him, kicking, squirming, threatening to kill him if he didn't let her go. Drew finally reached them and pulled Kate into his arms.

"Let me at him!" she screamed. When she saw Drew's eyes, her anger evaporated and she wrapped her arms around his neck, dissolving into tears. "I thought you were dead. But you're alive! I won't let him kill you. I won't!"

Carson sidestepped until she could see his face. "I'm not going to kill him, ma'am."

Kate snuffled into Drew's shirt. "You aren't?"

"No, ma'am. Drew explained what happened, the same as what you told me, and I believe him. Our business concerning Tom is done." Carson aimed his gun at the men on the porch, standing there like a couple of uninterested bystanders. "Except for these fellers, who don't know how to treat a lady."

Kate pulled free of Drew's embrace and ran toward the porch, where she stood between Carson and the two men. "Don't shoot."

Drew stared in disbelief. "Kate . . . ?"

Carson tilted his hat back on his head and gave Drew a look of sheer confusion.

"They're my brothers! Brothers I didn't know I had. They're the claim jumpers, only it's their claim, so I guess that means they aren't claim jumpers after all, since you can't jump your own claim. That means Pa is the claim jumper!"

"Claim jumpers?" Carson asked.

Drew shook his head. "It's a long story."

CHAPTER TWENTY-SEVEN

Back at the hotel, they found Caleb in the bar, drinking with May Belle or Pearl or whoever she'd decided to be today. When Drew, Kate, Carson, and the Mathison brothers appeared at the door, Caleb jumped up from the table, drawing his gun. He lowered it, though, when he saw four guns aimed back at him. Then he started laughing and hee-hawed until tears streamed down his face. "I swan. If the whole damned family isn't together at last. Come here, Katy darlin' and hug your old pa."

Kate stood where she was. "Why didn't you tell us we had brothers?"

Caleb stole a look at May Belle.

"Don't expect me to help you out of this one, you old coot. Tell her the truth for once."

"Yes," Kate said, pulling out a chair opposite her father. "The truth. For once."

Drew, Carson, and the Mathisons stood behind her. Drew rested his hands on her shoulders, sending tingles of desire through her in spite of the situation.

"Well," Caleb said, clearing his throat a couple of times, "after I left Sutterfield, I met this pretty young thing in Denver. She was as wound up about finding gold or silver as I was, so . . . well . . . I married her."

"Married her?" Kate thought she might explode. Anger filled her to the boiling point.

"Yep. Didn't tell her about your ma."

"Obviously." Drew squeezed Kate's shoulders and she hushed to let her pa keep talking.

"We had Sam and Joe, here. Milly died, God rest her soul, in a cave-in, two winters ago. That's when the boys decided the mine was theirs, since Milly had told them it would be theirs when we were gone." He glared at his sons. "When both of us were gone, you ungrateful—" Caleb started to stand, his hands balled into tight fists.

"We get the picture," Drew said. "So, why write to Ben and Kate?"

"I wanted my boys to see they had a brother and sister, so's they'd know the mine would belong to all of them—after I pass on to glory—which couldn't be too soon for them—and which could be any day now." He faked a cough.

May Belle cuffed his ear. "The truth, you old—"

"Ow! Cut that out, May Belle. I'm a dyin' man."

May Belle shook her head. "Only if being a sot will kill you any quicker than time itself."

Kate felt a sudden wave of sympathy for her pa. Where it came from, she couldn't imagine, until she realized the baby was kicking.

"Surely, you aren't going to die before you get to hold your grandchild." She felt Drew's hands tighten on her shoulders again and peered up at him. "Maybe Pa can hold out a few more months. What do you think, Drew?"

Drew took a long deep breath, then laughed with relief and happiness. Carson slapped him on the back.

"Why didn't you tell me?"

"You were so all-fired set on being killed, I didn't think you'd care," she lied.

Drew pulled her up from the chair and into his arms. Her impish grin made him smile.

"Let's go home to Texas, Miss Mathison."

"Whatever you say, Mr. Kingman."

ABOUT THE AUTHOR

Linda George has been a professional writer for more than twenty-five years. *Silver Lady* is her second novel for Five Star. She lives in West Texas with her husband, Charles, who is also a writer, and teaches sixth graders how to write. She's at work on a mystery and another historical romance. Linda's Web site is: www.SpotlightOnWriters.net